The Authentic Death of Hendry Jones

Charles Neider

APOLLO

Apollo Librarian | Michael Schmidt || Series Editor | Neil Belton
Text Design | Lindsay Nash || Artwork | Jessie Price

www.apollo-classics.com | www.headofzeus.com

First published in the United Sates of America in 1956
by Harper.

This paperback edition published in the United Kingdom in 2016
by Apollo, an imprint of Head of Zeus Ltd.

1 3 5 7 9 10 8 6 4 2

A CIP catalogue record for this book is available
from the British Library.

ISBN (PB) 9781784975135
      (E) 9781784975142

Typeset by Adrian McLaughlin
Printed and bound in Denmark by Nørhaven

Head of Zeus Ltd
Clerkenwell House
45–47 Clerkenwell Green
London EC1R OHT

W JM

APOLLO

To lovely Joan Merrick

1

Nowadays, I understand, the tourists come for miles to see Hendry Jones' grave out on the Punta del Diablo and to debate whether his bones are there or not; and some of them claim his trigger finger is not there, and others his skull; and some insist the spot is no grave, that it's just a little mound of abalone shells. Well take it any way you like.

There was a fellow came up to me one day and said, "You're Doc Baker I understand."

"That's right."

And without introducing himself he started pounding away at me.

"Now look Mister Baker," he said, "I saw a trigger finger in a bottle of alcohol back in Phoenix and there was a label on it and it said it was the Kid's finger. What do you say to that?"

"I say it's a damn fool who'll believe every label he reads," I said.

"Well that's all very well," he said. "But you tell me how it got there."

"Mister," I said, "I don't have to tell you anything."

"You're Doc Baker aren't you?" he asked.

"I am."

"Friend of the Kid's?"

"That's right."

"Well then," he said, looking up at me, being shorter than I.

"Mister your thinking has got itself shot up a little," I told him, "if you catch my drift."

"Well how did it get there?" he demanded. "And tell me this. What about the story he never got killed at all?"

"The Kid, my friend, is dead these many years," I said.

"Hmm," said the fellow.

"What's that?"

"Hmm."

"Oh. I thought you was cussing me out."

He looked at me queerly then, tipped his hat and walked off. And there was a fellow came up to me recently in the street and said, "You're crazy, Doc."

I looked at him closely and saw he was a stranger.

"Where's the Kid's skull?" he wanted to know.

"You damn fool," I said.

"You'll get yours one of these days," says he and disappears in the crowd.

Do you know where the old ghost tree on the Punta is? I don't mean the one overlooking the cove, the one so weather-colored, and wired against the wind and thieves, the one everybody goes to gawk at and which is within sight of the grave. I mean that other one just beyond the natural bridge under which the tide roars in and out, on the Punta's northern side, facing the old gaunt whitened rock rising out of the water like a great ship, where the gulls and cormorants nest. Well under that other tree, the ghost cypress rusting red on the bark and branches, is where we buried him and where he ought to be. But this was too far off the beaten path and dangerous for old folks and children because of the narrow way over the bridge and so they set up the stone marker by that other tree. That's the truth to the best of my memory.

And nowadays they talk of the Punta del Diablo as the Kid's Country, and Devil's Hill they call the Kid's Hill. The Kid would have gotten a kick out of that. He was always looking into newspapers and going off to a corner to read about himself, though I wonder if it's healthy for a man in his business to care what people think. And now the tourists come in the hope of finding some oldtimer to talk to about those days and to see the bullet marks on the town jail's walls and to see just where Patron fell and where Dedrick got the buckshot blast and to hear the stories about the women who were Hendry's sweethearts and the men his friends; and there are all these writers snooping around to find out what they can (and making up what they can't) and people complaining that no outlaw should have a stone over his grave, and you can buy a hundred guns supposed to have been his and run into fifty old geezers who have walked in from the deserts or hills claiming to be the Kid himself.

"I'm the Kid," one of them said recently. "I got all the markings to prove it."

"What markings?" we wanted to know.

"On my left leg and thigh. Acid burns."

"What burns?"

"Somebody spilled a bottle."

We looked him up and down and said, "Where you been all this time Kid?"

"Hear of Death Valley Scotty? Out in that part of the country."

"Sure enough. What made you come back?"

"Wanted to put things straight kind of."

"What you mean kind of?"

"Like I said."

"Now look mister," we told him, "there never was an acid mark on the Kid."

"You fellows will be sorry," says he, looking hurt.

"Not this time bum," we said. And with that he shuffled off.

Well the years have got to bring their changes and I don't mind. If that's what they want these days it's all right with me.

Now if you'll just be patient I guarantee you'll get your money's worth but it's the truth I'm getting at and if you're not interested I suggest you run along to the stores and pick up one of the little books full of lies about the Kid's life, written by some smart-aleck easterner that never sat in a western saddle, never smelled good horseflesh or a campfire dying in the hills and yet is ready to tell the country all about the Kid. I was there and I know what happened. With a little patience you will know it too before long, for what I aim to tell is exactly how and why the Kid died, when there was no reason for him to have died at all.

Some people have told me I ought to tell about the Kid's early life, who was his mother, who his father, where he went to school, how he killed his first man, how he got to be so good with the gun, the great fighters he met and knew, the women he had, the men he killed, the way he cleaned out the faro bank in the Angels that time. But I see no point in going into all that. If you don't know about it you can find it in ten or twenty books and anyhow I can't swear to the truth of it and a lot of it sounds like bull to me, such as his cleaning out the twenty Navahos around Gallup, his race to save his dying friend (no horse can run like that for so long), his love for his mother (he never talked much about her but I got the feeling he hated her) and much more that I'm glad I've forgotten. What I'm telling is what I actually know and I'm telling it to set the record straight before it's too late, although it may be too late already judging by how they've got his story running now.

There was this fellow I met in Watsonville one day and he says to me, "I understand Mister Baker that you're aiming to conconct a story."

"I'm not aiming to conconct anything sir," I says.

"About the Kid."

"I heard you the first time."

"Well that's what they say over in Castroville."

"I don't care what they're saying in Castroville sir," I said, "nor in Pacific Grove nuther."

"It's important to *me* what they say."

"I see."

"What I heard tell is you're going to cover the ground," he said.

"Amen," I said.

"Let's have a drink," says he.

"Here in Watsonville?"

"Hell," he said, "Watsonville's as good a place as any."

The Kid was considered in that time, and by men who ought to have known, by the only men who could judge such matters adequately, as the greatest gunman alive at the time of his death.

Take Dad Longworth:

"The Kid's in a class by himself."

Or Wyatt Earp:

"There never was a gunfighter like the Kid."

"What about Billy the Kid?" I once asked Wyatt.

"The Kid would have cut Billy in two."

"How about you Wyatt?"

He just smiled and shook his head.

Or take Buffalo Bill:

"I've known some galoots but none like the Kid. Best all-around gunman of my time."

"What gave him his class?" a fellow once asked him.

"Terrific nerve boy and a surefire finger."

"Eye?"

"He had it."

"Muscle?"

"Of a cat."

"Speed?"

"He had everything," Bill said, pulling at his goatee.

"Would he have made a good buffalo hunter?"

"Too light," Bill said quickly.

"Meaning?"

"The kick of the gun would have ruined him boy. You know how many buffalo I killed in my time?"

"Ten thousand," the fellow said.

"Come again."

"Twenty?"

"Once more."

"A hundred thousand."

"Don't be bashful son."

"A million?"

"That's right boy. That's it on the head."

That was old Bill for you.

Billy the Kid was already dead. Billy was fast on the draw and had great luck too but Hendry was very fast and had even greater luck and besides he was steady in a way Billy never was, steady in the way of Wyatt, capable of walking up to an armed mob and telling them off, then turning his back on them and walking away; capable of going up quietly to a fellow, yanking the fellow's gun and clubbing him with it. That was not the sort of fellow Billy was, although I'm not here to run Billy down.

Wild Bill Hickok was dead too. I don't say Hendry could have beaten Wild Bill but I do say that for two men of that class to have shot it out would have been suicide for both. The same thing would probably have happened if Hendry and Wyatt had fought it out, although I would have put my money on Hendry. Wyatt was very good and the most dangerous thing about him was his nerve but the Kid had nerve too and gunmanship and luck and he had what Wyatt didn't have: wild imagination that Wild Bill had and which made him unpredictable. I don't think any other gunfighter had it outside of those two. The men who judged these things knew what they were talking about and they decided that Hendry was the greatest gunman alive at his death and one of the very greatest that had ever lived. Which is about the way I would have put it too.

There were four of us then in that summer of 1883. There had been more of us only a little while before then, before Hendry's capture and trial, but after his capture most of us scattered and that, really, was the end of our gang, for afterward we only hung around waiting to go into business again but after the escape the Kid was too wrapped up in whatever was taking his mind off real work. Once there had been twelve of us, a great bunch of boys, and we could have licked any part of that country. We had enough guns and ammunition cached out in the hills to keep us safe half a year and we had spots up there from which we could pick off a small army with our Winchesters and Sharps guns. But when they got Hendry they scattered us. We were a good bunch all right. Most of our names you've never heard of. We got killed before we made a name for ourselves or got tired of being hunted and took off for good. But a lot of us were good boys and you could have fun with us all right.

We'd go to cockfights and to the bearbaiting fights in the hills and we'd drink and gamble and whore around and live on the fat of the land. When things were quiet we could always shoot up a town or pick a fight with someone we wanted to kill or start a stampede or a small war. We never thought that some day we would be slowing down and none of us ever thought, I reckon, that maybe we'd get killed. We acted as though we'd live forever and when one of us got killed he was so surprised it had happened to *him*. That was just one of the ways in which we were different from the Kid. The Kid was never surprised about getting killed, despite the way it happened. He knew he was going to get killed and was waiting for it, I think, the day and the hour, and would have been disappointed if it hadn't come.

I've had people ask me why we turned outlaw. I've had them come up and say, "Baker, what you want to be against law and order for?"

"Man who's against it? What you saying?"

"You are," this one fellow said.

"Were man," I said.

"Same thing."

"You're a damn fool if you don't mind my saying so," I said. "That was before the amnesty. The general pardon. I'm the hottest law and order man in the state."

"Is that so?"

"You can bet on it mister," I told him. But I don't think it made any difference at all.

Hell, we never *turned*. Those things just happened. One fellow went one way and another another and the first thing you knew one of them was called an outlaw and the other was running a faro bank and was protected by the sheriff and, if need be, the whole damned U.S. army. You must remember that in those times things weren't all figured out the way they are now. There were times for example when a rustler was not a rustler but a fellow who made a living rounding up unbranded strays and who was a good and necessary hand in the business—until somebody got it into his head that it didn't pay to have him around any more and passed a law and armed a lot of men and went sneaking around looking for branding irons that it was death from then on to have found on you. I never met one outlaw, including the Kid, who had studied to be one. But I will admit that once you became one you were likely to continue being one. And why not? Who wants to be fenced in if you don't have to be? There was plenty of stray beef around and plenty of loose money and land, and women for the asking. So that in a nutshell is the story of our turning outlaw and if it makes you unhappy why write me a letter and I'll see what I can do about it for you.

In that summer there were four of us, and Harvey French got killed by Longworth in an accidental shot meant for the Kid, and Bob Emory got killed by the Kid in about the only killing the Kid was ever sorry about. Which left just the Kid and me for the end.

About this fellow the Kid is supposed to have been afraid of just before his death: we may as well get that part of the record straight too.

There was this new kid coming up down around the Angels—and the thing of it was that he was killed by a third-rater a couple of months after Hendry was killed—and about the time Hendry was running downhill there was talk coming through about how great this new kid was, how he outclassed Hendry and was going to come north and finish him off. It got through to Hendry, for this new kid was all the talk at that time, the way a new boxer will be in these days, and although Hendry tried not to let it bother him I could see it had him thinking and that some of his thinking was not good. He was feeling old, although he was only twenty-five. The new kid was nineteen, fresh, very fast, with several killings to his credit and with little to lose in the way of reputation and therefore likely to be reckless and dangerous. His name was Andy Somethingorother (he didn't even stick around long enough to get properly remembered)—and he was flashy: a gunfanner, a two-gunman and a fellow who even tried hip-shooting when the mood hit him. People figured that Hendry was now rolling downhill (which was true) and that the new kid would take over. Hendry wouldn't talk, about it much but when he did he would say, "Well let him come. There's only one way to settle this kind of thing."

The rumor was that Hendry had lost his nerve. But as I said, this new kid turned out to be a bum who had had a streak of luck and he never got a chance to be killed by the Kid. Hendry must have known that tired and rundown as he was he could have killed ten such bums as that fourth-rate kid.

*

As for Dad Longworth, you know he'd been a pard of the Kid's a couple of years past in Arizona, that they'd rustled and lived together until Dad got the notion he had to be a sheriff, with a wife and kids, and so took off for the Monterey country, where he was not too well known in a bad sort of way. I figure, although I'm not sure of it, not having heard the Kid tell of it, that the Kid followed him out there to make him sorry he'd ever turned sheriff. That was the story as I heard it at the time and I have no reason to doubt it now. You can understand that the Kid's continuing to be in that territory was poison to Dad and that if he didn't clear him out pronto he would find his sheriffing days had disappeared from under him. He had met Hendry secretly several times and asked him to leave the country but Hendry had only smiled and said,

"It's a free country Dad." Dad had said,

"Look Kid I'm asking you to leave I'm not telling you to," and Hendry had said,

"I got some work to do here." Dad had said,

"Well think it over," and Hendry had said, smiling,

"Sure Dad why not?" but he had no intention of thinking it over, his mind being set on what he wanted to do.

And that's the way it went for a while. Meanwhile the ranchers told Dad to get the Kid out of there and Dad sent the Kid word he was going to get him, to which the Kid replied,

"Just come on and stop the jawing."

From then on it was war between them. But after the Kid's escape it was hot for Dad in that country and he sent the Kid word that it was him or the Kid. To which the Kid made no reply at all, only laughed in that strange way of his.

I can still remember the first time I saw him, in the spring of 1881. It was in the Gabilan hills near the Rancho Rincón de la Puente del Monte and I was camping out alone. I had a very good horse and two good ones besides and was about to make my supper under a live-oak tree when these four fellows rode up, one very big, unshaven, dirty, about thirty years old, with a heavy gruff voice, two others medium-sized ordinary-looking cowhands but rough-dressed, their horses sweating, and the fourth a small sandy-haired boy, all carrying Winchesters across their pommels and wearing two guns on their hips. I had been squatting over my manzanita fire, thinking of the quiet supper I was going to have and how it would be a good thing if I had some company that I could trust not to put a bullet into my back, and I had been squatting there fooling with the fire and thinking what good country this was, the hills golden and peppered with mesquite and live-oak, the sky blue and clean and the sun very golden, and thinking that I was going to enjoy what I was going to eat because I felt in very good health, when I had heard the horses coming up, and I had turned and seen four horsemen trotting toward me from the east. They made no sign as they came. They rode up to where I was and looked down at me, saying nothing. I had a funny feeling up my back as if I had made a mortal mistake and my mouth began tasting dry and bitter.

I said, "Hi. Join me in some chow." They said nothing, just

eyed my horses. The big fellow got down, hooked his thumbs into his gunbelt and spat into the fire.

"You don't want them horses," he said.

"You're mistaken," I said.

He went over to the two horses and took hold of the reins. I grabbed his shoulder and spun him around. He went for his gun but before it was halfway out he heard the click as I cocked mine and his hand let go in a hurry. He looked up at his friends. The boy was grinning.

"Go ahead Bob," he said. "Shoot him."

One of the others laughed.

"Go ahead Bob," said the boy.

The big fellow growled. The boy laughed a long and peculiar laugh. I watched them, thinking they would crack down on me and give me my death. The manzanita fire was smoking heavily. The big fellow started coughing. The boy laughed again.

"We don't want your horses," he said softly.

"Mister," I said, "get onto your horse."

"That was a fast draw," said one of the men.

The big fellow said, "What do you want for them?" in a voice that growled.

"They're not for sale," I said.

"Come on," said the boy, partly turning his horse.

"They're good horses Kid," the big man complained.

"Come on," said the boy and the man mounted.

"You the Kid?" I asked.

The boy smiled and looked at my gun.

"Put it away," he said. "We got no trouble with you." And he jumped down and came over to me.

I jammed the gun away, wondering if they would corpse me now. He was small, with soft cheeks and boyish eyes and a boy's quick body. When he walked he walked softly, like a cat, and his spurs clanked and the large rowels slowly turned. He had a funny smile, his mouth breaking into tight wrinkles and showing the teeth, his mouth doing that almost all the time when he spoke, so that I wondered if it smiled like that when he slept. The wrinkles were cut into his face and even when he was not smiling I could see the lines. I would not have guessed then that I would see that smile on him when he lay dead and that I would be with him at his wake, his last and best friend.

"If you're not busy why don't you join us?" he asked.

"How you know you can use me?"

"I can use you all right Doc," he said.

"How you know my name?"

"Heard you were around these parts. I heard what you look like. And there's no mistaking a draw like that."

"A deal," I said.

We shook hands. The Kid turned to the big fellow and said, "Bob rustle us up something to eat." I saw the big one didn't like that and I said, "Hell I'll do it Kid. Come on down boys and have some chow."

And that was how it began.

I watched him a lot after that. He was different all right. He was such a small fellow—it made you want to laugh to think of it. I remember the time at a baile when a big farmer who had had too much rotgut and who, being from up Oregon way, did not know him by sight, ambled over to him and said, "Sonny you sure are small. Where you come from they cut you so small?"

The Kid laughed in the man's face.

The farmer stared at him and said, "Why you runt. You aiming to get broke in two?"

Another fellow grabbed his arm and whispered in his ear. The Oregon man piped down and kept looking over his shoulder for the next half hour. He lit out after that and was never heard of again in those parts.

There was the other time when a fellow in a saloon, watching the Kid drink, came over and said, "You sure got a lady's hands boy."

Upon which the Kid threw his drink in the man's face. When the man went for his gun the Kid caught his gun hand, armlocked him to the door and shoved him into the street. The man came back with his gun in his hand and the Kid shot him through the arm. We wanted to know why he hadn't killed him but he just called for another drink and picked up the talk where it had left off. It was not like him to let a man live after a thing like that but you couldn't predict him.

We liked him for a lot of reasons. Some liked him because they were afraid of him, others because they admired him and still others because they hated him. But I think most were drawn to him because of his luck. You could not help wondering how a fellow could have such luck. I heard people say his kind of luck was the kind that comes once in a hundred years and that when it comes nothing can change it. Others said it was the kind that belongs to kids and later I heard them say he was a kid no longer. They had given him that monicker when he was just a boy and it was time he had gotten himself another, for the years had changed him, but he died with that name and would have kept it if he had lived to be eighty.

He was a wonderful horseman. He had a small and quick body for it. When his horse bolted or reared, bucked or slid, he was just part of him and the wilder the horse was the better he liked it, holding the reins in one hand, raising the other, smiling that smile and whooping. Most of the fellows thought no more of a horse than of a cow but he liked horses, the way a fellow will like a dog. He was different in that respect too.

I can still see him now, walking around the Punta, smiling, his hands in his back pockets, his sandy head hunched. He had a funny laugh. To hear it you'd think he had asthma or something. His mouth would draw back, his head would go up, and out of his mouth would come a wet longdrawn sound, the teeth bright and solid, the upper lip curled back, showing purple and looking blistered, and his face so red that you thought he was about to have a stroke. But there was nothing asthmatic about him and despite his hunched head and tight shoulders his chest was open and loose and you knew he was breathing well. He was in good shape when I first met him, although he had already begun to run down from bad living.

I can still remember him clearly: that slightly hunched stroll, that smile, the face that sunburned so easily (I think that was one of the reasons he liked the foggy Punta), the red-rimmed slate-colored eyes, the close-cropped small sandy head, the golden hair of his eyebrows and the golden hair that grew up from his chest to his throat, the milky fingers with the faint freckles, the smoky lips, dry and creased, the small ears hugging his head, his pointed chin, the way he walked on the outsides of his feet, his toes pointing outward, his high throaty drawling voice, the powerful curves of his arches, his milky muscular body, the light down on the back of his hands, the way when he laughed and flushed his eyes gleamed like white enamel buttons and his hair seemed brightly hay-colored.

Hell I could go on and on about him.

I joined up with them—I was a wild kid myself in those days—and we had some great times—rustling, fighting, shooting up towns we didn't like, doing just about what we wanted to and getting away with it. I was twenty then. My name was Edward Richard Baker (they called me Doc because I had once assisted a traveling dentist back around Albuquerque). My father was John Farley Baker, known as "Jimmy Boy," a smith in Las Cruces, New Mexico Territory, where I was born. He had emigrated from Ohio and married a girl in Santa Fe. I grew up in the Territory, learned to ride and shoot there, and had to beat it out of there after a scrape. Of schooling I had very little, about as much as a poor boy could get on the frontier; but I liked to read and my mother put some good books in my way, which started a habit ending by my becoming a self-taught as well as a self-made man. Which is nothing to brag about when I consider what I might have become in that place and time.

I was a tall husky fellow then, about six feet high, with light brown hair and blue eyes, in very good health. I remember I had a habit the fellows used to rib me about: when I walked I swung from side to side. Inasmuch as I had long legs for a rather skinny body my co-ordination was not too good for running and some of the fellows used to call me "Skeleton Man" but it was in fun. I remember too that I had trouble with my voice. It was hollow in sound and on the loud side and I tried unsuccessfully to change it. Which about winds up the picture of me at that time.

There are a couple of matters I ought to set straight before we get going. One of them was the Kid's capture. People have come up to me and said, "How come a fellow like the Kid allowed himself to get caught?" Well there wasn't much to it, it was just one of those things. We were breakfasting one cold morning in the early spring of 1883 in an old shack on a hill-side south of the Valley and the first thing we knew we heard Dad Longworth's voice call out, "We got you surrounded. Come out with your hands high."

We shot at each other for a while with nobody getting hurt and then we saw that Dad and his men had settled down for a long stay, long enough to starve us out. Even then we didn't quit but when our ammunition ran low and Dad shouted they would burn us to the ground there was nothing for us to do but come out, especially when he promised we wouldn't be shot down.

The Kid came out smiling and said, "Hi Dad. How are things? Pretty good for you I reckon."

"I reckon," Dad grunted.

"One thing I wish you'd tell me," said the Kid.

"What's that?"

"How'd you know we were here?"

Dad grinned and said, "A little bird told me."

"I'll bet," said the Kid.

And that was all there was to it. There were five of us in the shack. They had to let the rest of us go for lack of evidence but they kept the Kid on a warrant for an old murder. There was that trial in Salinas and he was sentenced to be hung. But that was only the beginning of it, as you know. It was a quick trial all right, with the result never in doubt. The Kid had killed many men. I don't know why they decided to hang him for the killing of Johnson, which was in self-defense. Except that they wanted to see him hang regardless and weren't particular about the charge. Johnson was a Monterey teamster. He had gotten drunk in a Monterey saloon and had approached the Kid, who had been drinking too, and told him he ought to be hounded out of that country. When the Kid told him to shut up Johnson had gone for his gun. After the Kid shot him in the head he had continued drinking and for an hour no one had gone up to the body, pretending it wasn't there. These details had come up at the trial, together with the interesting one, sworn to by witnesses who had not been in the saloon as well as by some who had, that Johnson had been killed while unarmed.

It was a quiet trial. The Kid said very little, just smiled, and his lawyer did not have his heart in the job. The crowd was very quiet. Some people commented on how the Kid did not look dangerous at all and how it was not possible he was such a desperate. They said he looked just like a kid and what a shame it was he had taken to such a bad way of life. The judge, a Salinas man, said it would have been better if he had tried to escape and gotten himself killed, because it would have saved the county money, but the Kid just grinned when he heard it, having plans of his own that didn't include getting himself killed just yet.

The morning after the sentencing they put him in a buckboard and brought him over to Monterey town, shackled hand and foot and dressed as usual. He had on tight-fitting black woolen trousers, of the kind we used to wear in those days, modeled, I guess, on the trousers the Spanish gents wore in that country, and black narrow-toed high-heeled boots, and a white soft-collared shirt and a wide black belt and a large black sombrero.

The stories you sometimes hear of how we used to dress in those days, looking like pigs, are mostly untrue. In the hills, of course, living out, hunting, camping, doing a cowhand's work, it was another matter, for then we were at work, wearing shaps, eating dust and not minding much how we looked. But in town and around the Punta we were always well dressed, taking a kind of pride in it, like the Spanish gents themselves, for we were not exactly working men but rather a kind, like gamblers, that lived off their wits. We rarely if ever lacked money for the things we wanted. We bought the finest boots and sombreros from down in old Mex and had hand-tooled saddles filigreed in silver and all the sorts of things that please a young fellow.

As for the Kid, he was the neatest of us all except when we were out on the range, and he always wore black except for his white shirts, and on more than one occasion I saw him in a black suit with a black string tie and a black top hat, and he cut quite a figure in those towns, dressed like that in the middle of the week and with his jacket always unbuttoned so that he could get at his forty-four without trouble if he wanted to.

When they brought him over from Salinas after the trial we were hiding out midway between the two towns—four of us—planning to give him a little reception. But the cover was bad, the hills naked, and when we saw how many men they had guarding him we put the notion of an escape out of our minds. They had two men riding up front and two covering the rear and one on each flank and these were special deputies, carrying their rifles where they would do the most good in the quickest time. Dad Longworth drove the pair of horses, with the Kid on the seat on his right, and behind them rode Pablo Patron and Lon Dedrick, with Dedrick just behind the Kid, his shotgun across his pommel. I figured Dedrick would kill the Kid before we had a chance to do a thing and even if I was wrong I knew we had no chance against that bunch and so we let them pass and thought of ways of rescuing him from the jail.

But we gave that up too. It's true Dad sent the six extra deputies away but we weren't sure of it, we thought they were planted in houses around the plaza; and anyway the lynch mob in town was armed and so were the Dedrick boys and we knew we would be slaughtered if we tried to come in there on them.

It was a very bright day when they brought him to the jail on that thirtieth of May. There were lots of people in the plaza waiting for a look at him, Nika Machado among them. He saw her in the crowd and waved. There were people milling around the jail door and kids running around on the plaza. Dad, I believe, expected us to try to take the Kid then and he also thought a mob would try to lynch him. Certain citizens had declared that lynching was the only just end for the Kid, inasmuch as Johnson had been a Monterey man and the Kid had been operating in the Monterey area. I don't know if the judge was in cahoots with them but he might have been. It was on their petition that he sentenced the Kid to hang in Monterey rather than in Salinas, where he already was.

But nobody tried anything. There were catcalls and whoops but nothing happened and the Kid seemed to be having a great old time. Dad went ahead of him into the jail, with Pablo just behind and with Dedrick behind Pablo. The six extra men covered the crowd with their rifles. Shortly after they disappeared inside, the Kid appeared at the front window of what was to be his cell, the southernmost room upstairs, facing the plaza, and he smiled and waved his shackled hands at the crowd.

2

He had followed Dad inside the jail and had at once begun making himself familiar with it. He knew it in a general way, the way he knew Pablo and Lon and Charley's across the plaza, having been inside it a couple of times but not for incarcerating reasons. He entered the vestibule and began following Dad up the stairs.

"What's up? Why upstairs?" he asked. He knew the cells were on the ground floor.

Dad turned and smiled. "We got a special room for you."

"Any other prisoners?"

"Three."

"Downstairs?"

"Yep."

"No company."

"No company."

It was a steep flight and not easy to manage with irons on his hands and legs but he pretended it was harder than it was. He gripped the banister and pulled himself up. Dedrick had gotten behind him. He shoved him hard in the back with the muzzle of the shotgun. The Kid was surprised, thinking that Pablo was still behind him and not believing that Pablo would do a thing like that. Turning around, he saw Dedrick's grinning face and, gripping the banister, swung his legs into the air and dug his heels into Lon's chest. Dedrick staggered and let out a bellow. He threatened the Kid with the shotgun but Dad had spun around and drawn. Dad said flatly, "None of that," and Lon lowered the gun and complained of what the Kid had done.

"Why'd you do it?" asked Dad.

"He rammed that thing into my back," the Kid said mildly.

Dad looked at Dedrick. "How come you're behind him? I thought Pablo was behind him. Lon you try anything—"

"What's the matter? He a friend of yours?"

"Why you shit, he's more a friend of mine than you are," Dad said and continued up the stairs.

The Kid was thinking. Past the stairs on the ground floor you came to a corridor. The first door on your left was Dad's office. The door on your right was another office. It was through this one you went when you went to the yard. Beyond Dad's office was a cell. Across from it another cell. And if he remembered right there was a small one, rarely used, just back of the stairs.

When he reached the top of the stairs he followed Dad down the corridor, passing a door on each side, and stopped as Dad pushed open the last door on the left. He went inside and Dad followed him.

"Watch out for that son of a bitch," Dad said in a low voice. "If it's all the same to you I want you to be on hand Saturday morning."

"Why don't you get rid of him?"

"I can't. The whole county'd be against me if I did. They're already saying I got no business keeping a greaser on this job and that I was once a friend of yours and would like to see you escape. Don't rile him. I'm going to get rid of him soon as this is over."

"I'd like to stick around just long enough to kill old Lon."

"Well see he doesn't kill you first."

Dad locked him in. The Kid went to the window and looked at the crowd. He watched the plaza and One-eyed Charley's and the crooked streets beyond Calle de Estrada and the smoke rising from the white adobes. Then he went to the other window. A street, some houses, a couple of stray dogs, lots of morning sunlight. Bars on his windows. He turned to look at the room. Not much to look at. A bunk near the plaza window, an old scarred table, one chair, a fireplace on the right of the door as you came in. Between the two windows a brown chest with an ironstone pitcher and bowl and no doubt a chamber pot inside. An old unsilvering mirror above the chest, an oil lamp and an abalone shell ashtray on the sill. The floor of heavy oak planks, unevenly stained. The walls formerly whitewashed but now the gray and brown adobe showing through. A small square room where he would have a little more than four days to live.

He got up and stretched to get rid of the buckboard

stiffness. The shackles clanked. Whatever he would do those shackles would clank. He lay down on the bunk and fell asleep, dreaming of Dad. Dad was helping him to escape, was giving him guns and horses and even a cannon.

A key was thrust into the lock, the lock was turned and the door opened into the room. The Kid awoke and saw Pablo standing in the doorway, covering him with his forty-five. Dedrick stood behind him in the corridor, the shotgun ready. Dedrick was a big fellow and heavy, with a large face and a bull neck, a short upturned nose and eyebrows that slanted down to meet at the bridge of his nose. He walked with a swagger, wore his dark hair long and wore two guns. Sometimes, seeing him ride, you'd think you were looking at a traveling arsenal. He'd be wearing his six-shooters, would have an extra one slung over his pommel, and would carry a Winchester rifle and a shotgun.

"What's up?" asked the Kid.

"Lunch," Pablo said.

He went and brought it: enchiladas, frijoles and coffee. The Kid ate it sitting on the bunk. Pablo sat on the chair opposite him while Dedrick stood in the doorway, watching.

"Hungry?" asked Pablo.

The Kid was silent.

"That's all you get," Pablo said.

"It'll do."

"Maria Jesús … she's going to bring me mine soon. You want some?"

The Kid looked up at him. "She your wife?"

Pablo nodded.

"I got enough. Didn't know you were married."

"I got three kids," said Pablo, smiling.

"Great," said the Kid, wiping his mouth with the back of his hand. "I never married."

"I know."

"Now it's too late—or is it?" The Kid threw his head back and laughed.

Pablo laughed too, tentatively at first. Dedrick glowered.

"What's eating Lon?" asked the Kid.

"I tell you what's eating me," Lon said. "We ought to kill you now and save the county money."

"What you got against me friend?"

Dedrick spat into the room.

The Kid sniffed and said, "I smell piss. You smell piss Pablo?"

Pablo laughed and glanced at Dedrick. Dedrick said, "You just wait."

"Lon's pissed on himself again I reckon," said the Kid dryly.

The thing you noticed about Dedrick was that he smelled of urine. I don't know what caused it. We none of us bathed too often but we had no urine smell on us. Lon almost always did. I reckon it was some trouble he had with his kidneys or bladder.

"How your brothers?" asked the Kid. "Still live on the hill with them?"

Lon didn't answer.

"Lon's mad at me," said the Kid. "When's your wife coming?"

"In a little while," said Pablo. "Why should I pay to eat over at Charley's?"

"Where you live?"

"Calle de Estrada."

"Lucky. Save you money."

"You bet."

The Kid wiped his mouth on his sleeve. As he did so he struck the tin coffee can with his elbow and spilled it. Pablo had to go for a rag to wipe it up.

"Why don't you help him?" the Kid asked Lon.

Lon spat into the room again.

"I'm sorry," said the Kid when Pablo returned.

"That's all right."

"It's the irons."

"Sure."

Dad called Lon and Lon disappeared. Pablo went to the window and said, "Play lots of cards hey Kid? Kill time."

"Why not."

"Friend Nika Machado was here."

"Oh yeah?"

"Dad said no visitors today. But she can come tomorrow. I thought—"

"She coming?"

"I don't know…. One thing I do know. Dad's worried."

"What about?"

"That lynch mob."

"Fourflushers," said the Kid.

"No. I know them. Dad says they may come tonight. If not tonight then tomorrow."

"What's he aiming to do?"

"You got me."

"Three kids ... Nice?"

"The best."

"Too bad I'll never see them."

"You can if you want. They'd like— Be all right?"

"Sure."

"This afternoon?"

"Sure."

"Been bothering me about it. All the kids in town want to meet you."

"I'm a shining example."

"Lon's taking the prisoners over to Charley's."

The Kid stood up and they looked at the plaza and watched Lon and the three men. Pablo's hand was on his gunbutt, ready for trouble. He was a small fellow but dangerous, fast on the draw and a good shot, much better with a sixgun than a rifle.

"You don't have to do that," the Kid said.

"You're wrong," said Pablo. "A man will do anything to save his life. I like you ... but I can't trust you. Not now. It's my life against yours."

He had dark shiny hair and dark eyes with whites that seemed dark too and a small face with fine features and a satiny brown skin. Small-hipped, partly bowlegged, with almost no bottom at all. A neat fellow in tight black trousers, high-heeled black boots and soft gray shirt.

"I reckon you're right hombre," said the Kid. He sat down on the bunk while Pablo carried the board with its dishes out into the corridor and locked the door.

The Kid lay on his bunk, smiling, thinking of nothing, enjoying his lunch. He rose and rapped on the door.

"Hombre!"

Pablo asked, "What's up?"

"Outhouse." Pablo opened up and followed the Kid down the corridor and down the stairs and through the little office into the yard.

"You know your way around," he said.

"Been here a couple of times."

"Good memory."

The Kid laughed. He held out his wrists. Pablo unshackled them. Then he went inside and sat down. When he came out Pablo shackled him again. The Kid looked around the yard. An old adobe wall more crumbling than not, the outhouse on the right, the stable on the left. An untended yard, the weeds, grass and shrubs growing wild. Near the stable an old wooden gate, and in the back of the yard a larger gate, or what had once been a gate, for now only some old planks remained, hanging on to large rusty hinges. A man could not hope to escape by either gate if he wore irons and was on foot. With a horse, however, he might have some kind of a chance.

He returned to his cell. As he sat down on his bunk Dad poked his head into the room to take a look around, then disappeared, and Pablo locked the door on the outside. In a little while he opened it again to let a woman in. She carried a straw bag. She was small and a little plump and had a clear brown skin, large eyes, a flat nose and beautiful black hair which she wore in a bun on her nape.

"My wife," said Pablo.

"Maria Jesús," said the Kid, standing up.

She smiled and showed good teeth. Pablo locked the door on the inside.

"I brought you some food," she said. "And Pablo his lunch."

"What you got? Pablo told you I just had my lunch?"

"Was it enough?"

"It was all right."

"I have tortillas and some soup with meat."

"The county's paying to feed me. I get enough. Sit down?"

He offered her the chair and she accepted it, setting the bag on the floor beside her. She used her eyes freely while talking and her voice was husky and a little flat and nasal.

"Charley's food is garbage," she said. She turned to Pablo. "How would you like to eat that food?"

"Lon likes it," Pablo said.

"That slob would like I don't want to say what," she said, frowning.

The Kid laughed. "This is funny," he said.

"What?" asked Maria Jesús.

"You bringing me food."

"You want to insult me?"

"Who? Me?"

"Then why you say that? I know how they feed you fellows. I'll bring you more tomorrow. Pablo comes home for dinner so I can't bring you dinner but he can bring you something. At least I can bring you lunch. Tomorrow a little wine. It will make you happy."

"This hombre's always happy," said Pablo.

The Kid laughed. "Why not? One life. Or is there another?"

"Don't talk like that," she said.

"No? Teach me. Pablo's a deputy. He'll watch me hang on the fourth. You coming to the show?"

The Kid laughed.

"You ought to be ashamed," she said, frowning.

"Why? It's public."

"When they bring the priest will you be kind to him?"

"Sure. But I won't listen."

"You must."

"No," he said dryly, turning partly away from her, "it's not for me. I've lived without them and I can die without them."

"It's terrible to go like that."

"One way's as good as another."

"It's because you never married and had children."

"I'd still not mind the going."

"You'll try to escape?"

The Kid smiled and glanced at Pablo.

"If I get the chance."

"If you try—don't hurt Pablo. He's a good man. And you must listen to the priest."

"Sure. Sure."

"I'm sorry for you."

"What's there to be sorry about?"

"Your soul."

"No better be sorry for this body. There's at least another year in it."

"You're joking. I hope I have not disturbed you. Will you take my food?"

"Thanks."

"I'll leave it here in the bag."

"Thanks."

"Goodbye. May God forgive you."

"God has nothing to do with it. Goodbye Maria Jesús."

It was about one o'clock now, a little past siesta time. The Kid fell asleep. He slept deeply, without dreaming, awoke in about an hour, got up, rummaged in the bag Maria Jesús had left, found a jar of soup, lifted it to his mouth, fished some pieces of meat with his fingers and ate them, wiping his hands on his trousers. As the soup and meat settled he began to feel sleepy again. He rolled a cigarette and lit it. The window was partly open. He went to it and opened it wide. No one on the plaza. He breathed in the air and tested the bars. They were set firmly. He returned to the bunk and soon fell asleep again. Again he did not dream.

When he awoke he judged it to be about three. He rapped on the door. No answer. Then Dedrick's voice said sleepily, "What you want?" "Outhouse." Dedrick opened the door and followed him out of the house into the yard. When the

Kid lingered Dedrick shoved the muzzle of his shotgun into his back. The Kid spun around to face him and saw Dedrick grinning at him, aiming the gun at his stomach and playing with the triggers.

"Why don't you make a break for it?" Dedrick said softly.

The Kid smiled. "I'm not aiming to make it easy for you Lon boy."

"Go ahead. You're so brave."

"No you're the one."

"They're coming for you tonight."

"Let them," said the Kid. He held out his wrists for Lon to unshackle them.

"Don't stick your paws at me," growled Lon. But he unlocked the shackles and removed them, doing it with one hand while holding the shotgun with the other.

The Kid went inside the outhouse. He did not really have to go. He had made the trip for the exercise and to see what he could learn, but mainly he had made it to establish a pattern of going there several times a day.

When he returned to his cell the door was open. Pablo and his three boys were waiting for him, Dad with them. They were young, the oldest being about eight. Thin and brown and short-haired, with their mother's large eyes. They wore cheap white shirts and blue cotton trousers. Pablo introduced them. The oldest boy asked, "You afraid?"

The Kid laughed and said, "I sure am."

The boy looked puzzled. Pablo said, "He's not. He's joking."

"That true?" the boy asked.

"Your father's the one who makes the jokes. A great hombre your father."

"Where's your gun?" the middle boy asked.

"They took it away."

Dad smiled and winked. Pablo was grinning. Lon shuffled out of the room and down the stairs.

"You killed many men?" the oldest boy asked.

"No. Not any."

Pablo laughed. "You believe everything he tells you?"

"They're going to hang you Saturday," the middle one said. "Can we shake hands?"

"Sure," said the Kid, and he shook hands with each of them.

"All right kids let's go," Pablo said. And he hustled them out of the cell, leaving with them.

"You expecting trouble this evening?" the Kid asked Dad.

"Maybe."

"What you going to do if they come?"

Dad scratched his head. "I don't know."

"Look out you don't get yourself lynched." The Kid laughed.

"What you got to be laughing about?"

"It's funny."

"What?"

"Everything. Where's your sense of humor?"

"I must have lost it somewhere."

"Now don't go and get sour on me."

Dad eyed him. "You sure are a card," he said and left the room, locking him in.

*

The two prisoners in the cell below were arguing loudly. The Kid went to the plaza window and looked out, rolling a cigarette. The two-story adobe cast its shadow onto the lawn. Suddenly he stamped his heel several times against the floor. The noise below stopped at once. A little later he heard whispering down there. He went to the door and tried the knob. Strong. The door heavy. He returned to the window. The afternoon light was growing yellow. He thought of Nika Machado.

There was a rap on the door and Dad opened it. Lon stood in the doorway, the shotgun ready. Dad sat down, the Kid standing with his back to the window. Dad said there was a fellow downstairs, a merchant he called himself, who wanted to know if the Kid had anything to sell. He wanted to buy the Kid's forty-four, his rifle if any, his gunbelt, and any odds and ends he had left. He would buy the clothes too, at a fair price.

"He wants the gun with the notches," Dad said, grinning. "He was sure disappointed when I told him you never notched your gun. What do you want me to tell him?"

"Tell him—"

"Me? That kind of language?"

"Your own then."

"I'm clean-mouthed—"

"Sure … What you want to get married for?"

"You can't go on living alone forever."

"Who wants to live forever?"

"I do," said Dad.

"Well I won't be around to see you when you're old and gray."

"You should have got married yourself."

"To slow me down?"

"How long you aim to keep running?"

"Another year or so." The Kid laughed.

Dad shook his head. "Your running days are over Kid …
A little poker tonight?"

"Sure. Why not?"

"Anything you want?"

"Yeh."

"Name it."

"A double-barreled shotgun and Lon in here alone
with me."

Dad laughed and stood up.

"You hear that Lon?" he asked.

Lon made a face. They locked the Kid in and clattered in
their high heels down the corridor and down the stairs.

He lay down on the bunk, then sat up and tried the leg irons.
Could he get hold of a file? How? What was next door?
Another cell? In what room did they keep their guns? Every
jail had a gunroom. What was in the room across the corridor? And in the small one opposite the stairs?

He studied his white shirt. Dirty. His black woolen trousers, which fitted snugly around his hips, were dirty too.
He had had a handkerchief. Had lost it somewhere. He
was beginning to stink. His sombrero was streaked with
dust. He must ask Pablo to have Maria Jesús brush it and
must ask Nika to bring him a fresh shirt and trousers. He

must have somebody polish his boots. He went to the pitcher and washed his face and hands in the bowl and dried them with a towel he found hanging on a nail inside the low chest, beside the chamber pot. Having to urinate, he got out the pot and went to the corner on the left of the door, farthest from the windows. He washed his hands again and flicked the towel at his boots and at his sombrero. Sitting down on the bunk, he rolled himself a cigarette with one hand and lit it with a sputtering sulphur match.

Pablo came in and showed him an old deck of cards.

"Poker?"

"Great," the Kid said. They began to play, Pablo sitting on the chair and keeping his hands low, so that his right hand would not have to travel far toward his gun.

"You any money?" he asked.

The Kid nodded and squinted through the smoke that rose up against one eye. They were playing with chips.

"Dad knows where my money is," the Kid said. "Don't worry. My credit's good. He'll pay you."

They played stud.

"I can't make you out," Pablo said.

"What am I supposed to say to that?"

"Me I wouldn't feel so good in your boots."

"You're not in my boots," said the Kid, studying his cards. Pablo was dealing.

"No."

"You're on the other side."

"Nothing wrong in that."

"No?"

"What?"

"Don't ask me. It was you who said it."

Pablo shook his head, puzzled. "I been thinking about it but I can't make you out."

"Don't strain it."

"Christ I got to get you your dinner. We'll play after dinner."

"When do you get yours?"

"When Lon comes back."

"Good. We play."

Pablo brought him the dinner and they played until Lon returned from Charley's. Pablo left for the night.

The Kid, alone, went to the plaza window, then came back to the bunk. He fell asleep. When he awoke it was night. He went to the window again and watched the moon. He wished he could see the bay. He thought of Nika. Figures on the plaza. They moved away. No lynching tonight. Dad came in and they played draw poker, Dad winning.

"What time is it?" asked the Kid.

Dad looked at his vest watch. "Almost nine."

"I'm going to turn in."

Dad left. The Kid lay down. He thought of nothing, just lay there with his eyes half open, watching the ceiling. Then he fell asleep.

3

You'll hear people say Dad Longworth was a great sheriff, also a great gunfighter, a greater fighter than the Kid. That's hornswoggling. He was an honest sheriff, I'll say that for him. And he was no coward. You don't find many fellows like the Kid, who don't have nerves at all and who like to risk it for the hell of it and to test their luck. Dad knew he stood a good chance of being killed by the Kid, but it didn't keep him from going after him after the Kid skedaddled. He was a fellow who knew his duty. You might say his having a wife and two kids made all the difference. Maybe. But I've known plenty of sheriffs who were dishonest and who had more kids than Dad ever had.

As for his being a great gunfighter, he was not a bad one, you understand, but not in the Kid's class. His luck happened to be very good when they met in Hijinio Gonzales's adobe that moonlit August night. It was nothing you could have planned. It is just plain stupid to believe he lay in wait for the Kid to ambush him. He was doing his duty and the Kid walked onto him. Luckily for Dad he was in the pitch-blackness of Hijinio's room when the Kid walked in and the moonlight was behind the Kid and on his legs and that was all there was to it. Once the Kid sensed there was someone in the room besides Hijinio, Dad was a dead man if he didn't shoot first. That was the way the play went and there's no changing the falling of the cards.

Even Dad himself used to say afterward, "It was pure luck boys. For a minute my spine said, 'Dad you're going to get it,' but before I knew it I had shot him. Hell nobody knows that better than me."

"Tell me this," somebody once said. "Did the Kid have a gun?"

Dad shook his head angrily and said, "Boy you're sure going to make me mad. There were *witnesses*. Sure he had a gun. I could see it glinting in the moonlight. He had a gun and a meat knife and I could see both of them glinting. Besides I'd have shot him anyway, just on the chance he had one. What would you have done? Come to think of it you wouldn't have been there in the first place would you?"

"I'm not a sheriff."

"I guess you're not."

"Hell Dad I didn't mean no harm," said the fellow. "I was just asking. And I'm not the only one."

"That's just it. You're not," said Dad angrily.

As I say I didn't know him very well but we knew each other by hearsay and that was a lot. Practically everybody knew everybody else in that way in those times.

I once said to him, "Dad what was the Kid like in the old days?"

He screwed his face up in that way of his, frowning hard, and shrugged.

"He a crack shot?"

"Sure. At fourteen," he said.

"When he kill his first man?"

"Fool me."

"Pretty young?"

"So they say."

"You're not sure."

"Look I've heard too many sides. I'll tell you this: he was always good. Even when I met him. A nicer kid then come to think of it. Didn't care about a thing except to laugh and raise hell and whore around. He's changed. Who hasn't? Me I had enough of that life. Fellow has got to settle down. Take the Kid."

"Not the type."

"I want to have an old age."

"What you want to be sheriff for then?"

"It's not that bad. Times are changing."

"Yeh I guess they are at that."

I remember the first thing I noticed about him—his posture: his broad almost rigid back, heavy neck, and the sort of rigidity of movement in his whole body. I understand he had been sickly as a child and had gone in for exercise and in his youth had worked on a river boat loading bales. At the time I knew him he was still very strong, too strong for his present work, so that sometimes he complained his muscles ached just from want of something to do. I remember also the two great silver rings he wore on the index and middle fingers of his left hand and his huge silver buckle with the chunk of polished jasper in the middle. The rings had ovals of polished agate. He had made them all himself back in the Navaho country. The rings were really tremendous and they seemed to dwarf even Dad's huge rough hairless hands.

When I first met him he was sitting behind a table in a saloon in Salinas and I thought, Jesus this is a big boy. But when he stood up I saw he was only of middle height, shorter than myself, for his legs were short, and bowed at that. And he was nervous: his hands shook slightly when he rolled and lit a cigarette and he frowned heavily whenever he spoke. As a matter of fact he had difficulty speaking as I recall, except when he was joshing somebody or being joshed. I never met a man who liked joshing the way he did. His hair was light brown and wavy, his eyes a dirty blue, and his heavy face was seamed and brown. He was in good shape, all right, and fairly quick on the draw, and good in the saddle and a good all-around cowhand. Too bad he got killed that way.

Dad was part Navaho and proud of it, although aside from his heavy cheekbones there was little Indian to see in him. His wife was Mexican and his kids very dark and pretty. They spoke Mexican better than they spoke English. Dad spoke Spanish pretty well himself and some Navaho too and he was happy with his wife and two boys over in Salinas. He was older than most of us, being then about thirty-two or -three, and intent on making a good settled life for himself. I think he planned on going into some business for himself and there was no reason why he couldn't have succeeded.

He liked to kid you at any time of day or night. He liked to come up and shout, "Hi Doc what's up?" and slap you on the back and tell you about his pappy back in Dodge City and how his pappy had an old muzzle loader that he shot from his porch at the rabbits.

"Are you really part Indian?" I once asked him.

"You bet boy," he said. "You can see it can't you damn it?"

"I guess I can at that."

"Hell if you know Indians you can. What's the matter? You don't look so snappy today."

"Maybe there's a reason for it."

"Reason? Go on."

"Maybe it's because I don't *feel* so snappy."

He laughed and clapped me on the shoulder.

"Hell boy," he said, "even I don't feel so snappy now and *then*."

He was built like a rock and I doubt he ever had a bad day but for some reason he was nervous. When he'd be shaky somebody would say, "How you doing Dad?"

"Not so good."

"What's the trouble?"

"Not my day I reckon."

"What you been up to?"

"Not a thing. That's what makes me so damned mad."

"Take it easy boy."

"Hell that's what I'm trying to do," he would say.

In a way it was too bad Whitey Pearce went and killed him, for Dad was not a bad fellow, not half as bad as some of the fellows who went on living year after year. I hated him for a while after he killed the Kid but I was never one to hold that grudge against him, seeing as how I knew it was more the Kid's fault than Dad's and seeing as how Dad had no choice in the matter anyhow. I think the Kid liked him and I understand Dad really liked the Kid, and the only sorry thing about it was that they were no longer operating on the same side. Dad's wife married again the year after he was killed. A woman didn't believe in being a widow for long. She needed a man to protect her and to take care of her kids. She married a fellow, I heard, who had never been married before and folks said it was decent of him to marry her, her with the two boys. But then she was a pretty girl and still young and it was a Mexican who married her and I understand she was very strong and worked well in the fields.

As for Lon Dedrick, he was just a loudmouthed fourflusher and about as dangerous, out in the open, as a kingsnake, but we knew from experience a fellow like that could be dangerous in the dark corners. He was the kind that operated best when a man's back was turned or when the man was unarmed or shackled. I wonder if there was a man alive outside of his two brothers who had any use for Lon. Lon was just plain lowdown and the whole town thought so. But they gave him leeway in memory of his father, who had been a butcher in town and had died about five years before from a stroke, and because of his mother, a quiet churchgoing woman who now lived alone and supported herself by doing odd chores and by laundering for a few of the good families. Even his mother had no use for him. After Lon was killed a couple of women went to tell her about it and she said, "I'm glad. That boy was no good. I'm sure he's gone straight to hell." It got around town and shocked a lot of people and set a lot of others to laughing. The truth was, lots of people felt that way about Lon's death and lots of them said so, but no one expected a fellow's own mother even to think it, much less say it. That was the sort of fellow Lon was and that was the kind of mother he had.

The family had come out from Georgia when Lon was about ten and had come straight to Monterey because the father had a cousin there, who shortly afterward removed and died. Back in Augusta the father had had himself a meat store and they had struggled along. Lon was no good from the start. He had been larger and heavier than most of the kids his age and had long ago got himself a reputation as a bully. He had had a third brother, who had been killed in a fall from a horse during a roundup in Texas. As a kid Lon had worked in his father's store in Monterey but then had gone off to work on the nearby ranchos, where he was not a bad cowhand. How he got to be a deputy I don't know, but it doesn't matter—anybody at all could get to be a deputy in those days. He had killed a couple of men but I think it was always without giving them a fair break. Once he walked up to a fellow he was supposed to be friendly with but who had rubbed him the wrong way the day before and he said, "Hello Ace" and stuck out his hand to shake hands. He caught the fellow's right hand with his left, jerked his gun and killed him. The Kid would sometimes taunt him by saying, "The only men you ever killed were shot in the back. Why don't you reach for your gun?" But that was when the Kid was free. Now it was a different story.

He was sure one lunkhead, with his horseteeth and his self-satisfied grin and the way he had of shaking his head from side to side when he talked and not looking into your eyes, and laughing first at his own jokes, and bragging about the women he had, and that curl of his lips when he smiled, and those murky eyes and wet hands, and his bad feet and the way his dark hair grew low down on his forehead, and his claims to being a badman. They sure rang no bells in that town when Lon took off.

As for Pablo Patron, I never did know much about him. I know he lived in a small adobe on the southern edge of town, with a yard full of mission figs and sunflowers, and that he liked his job and that Maria Jesús washed clothes for some of the white families, and I guess Pablo hoped some day to be a full sheriff, maybe down in some smaller town or down in old Mex—but that's about all I can remember about him, although I probably knew much more back in those days.

It was quite a town, that town the Kid was jailed in and was due to hang in. Not like Salinas—dry, dusty, nothing but fields around it, away from the sea and with nothing elegant going on. A good town, lying between the horns of the bay, its whitewashed adobes gleaming in the sun. Much of it poor—shacks of fishermen and of the Chinese colony that shipped dried abalone home, and of the whaling men and miners who worked in the inlets and hills. Streets narrow and dirty, muddy in a rain. The broader ones avenues of dust in the dry season, with a few horses waiting with lowered heads, and natives squatting in the shade or peering from behind adobe walls: these and the hangdog-looking dogs.

What would a young fellow find to interest him in a town like that? Well it wasn't everywhere you could find sailors and ships and fishermen. And although there were fine haciendas in the hills they couldn't sport, even the best of them, the kind of houses you saw in Monterey town or the quiet company or the gardens, the walls of fuchsias, the espaliered trees, the moss-grown brick walks, the pepper trees, willows and Japanese plums, the acacias, the adobe walls topped by tile, the bits of whalebone sidewalk, gray and webby. You always found the finest things in town: Chinese teakwood tables with marble tops, Japanese tortoiseshell bowls with eagles and herons inlaid with gold; English ironstone china; mantillas of Chantilly lace; the mantones de Manila, the Spanish shawls embroidered in China and brought across the Pacific by way of the Philippines; satin dolmans worn over taffeta gowns; Dutch and English clocks; and all the rest of such stuff.

It was good to sit in that town after the hills and Punta, to sit in a plaza and listen. Cries on the bay; bark of a dog; rattle of carts; clopping of hooves; voices laughing and shouting. It made us wonder how it would be to live in a place like that, with all the houses and faces and business and all the smells—grapes being pressed, eucalyptus trees, pine smoke, roses, meat curing, cheeses drying, and the perfume you caught as you passed a lady on the street.

It was good too to ride toward town from the Punta, taking Devil's Hill slow through the pines and enjoying the bay like a saucer ahead of us, the adobes glowing in the light, the yellow sandhills running north, the pines speckled above, the clouds lying over Santa Cruz in the far distance, and the whole thing obscured by patches of gray fog which crept or scudded. And good too to lean back in the saddle and stretch our legs against the wooden stirrups and smoke a fresh-rolled cigarette and feel our horses under us, taking their time, looking around to study something, twitching their ears and neighing, sighing now and then as if they'd worked all day, and smelling strong of sweat and fields and hard-worked leather.

You understand that when we went into town in the later days it was not by invitation. To show you that town had class all I have to say is they didn't run or hide but went about their business, knowing how to do business with everybody, even those who wore guns. The law said you had to leave your guns outside of town but we wore them on our hips and stuck them in our saddles. To do anything else might have meant an ambush or we might have been shot down right on the Calle Principal. I'm talking about the time before the Kid's escape; after it we could not have gone in unless we had a cannon with us.

We would walk down the Calle Principal or the Calle de Alvarado and study the shops. We liked to go down to the Customs House and lounge under the portico or visit the Washington Hotel for a supper with trimmings—linen, silver, fingerbowls—or Simoneau's for something Frenchy, and sometimes it felt as though we were the only ones on foot in that town, for most everybody rode, even if it was only a couple of streets they had to go. We knew it was not a great town. We had been to Frisco and had seen the difference. But it was a good town and had been a great town in its time, in the days of the Spaniards. The gold rush had ruined it but it was a matter of opinion what you meant by ruined. Some people, the traders, thought it had been ruined but others, such as the natives, thought it had been saved. A quiet town, although once in a while somebody like Tiburcio Vasquez or Joaquin Murietta or the Kid stirred it up a little.

We had a couple of friends over on Calle de Montenegro and would go there to dine, as you might say, two of us guarding the front and back of the house. A fine house of two stories, with a dance room downstairs and a billiard room upstairs and a chamber pot in every room. Heavy timbers in the ceilings and wide oak boards, adzed and stained, on the floors. Walls four feet thick. A carriage house, stable, garden. Blackberries and mission figs in the garden as well as a plum and an apple tree and a grape arbor, all smelling of herbs—camomile, lemon verbena, sage, rue, lavender. Sometimes we spent a night there. I had a little room with wide milled boards painted white, one window with square panes and a thick ledge, a low chair with a cushion center, a wooden bedstead, a fireplace, a small hip-high green cabinet, an embroidered footrest, an oil lamp and a white washbowl and pitcher. Chinese straw matting on the floor. On one wall a painting—of a yellow-haired girl in a white dress with a high waist and naked shoulders, wearing white stockings and high black boots. She sat beside a fawn. In her left hand she held some red and yellow roses. Her face looked frozen and stupid.

Quite a place. The owner was a great admirer of the Kid and did a lot of business with him in counterfeit money. I sure liked to go there and have my enchiladas brought to me by a native girl. Good life we had then. You can see I haven't been lying. Good town as towns went—but now the Kid was due to be hung in it and he was due to be hung on Saturday morning and here it was already Monday night.

4

Tuesday morning slipped by and before the Kid knew it it was siesta time and then siesta was over and in the middle of the afternoon Dad came in to say that there was a newspaper fellow downstairs who wanted to interview him and that if the Kid agreed it was all right with him. The Kid smiled and said, "What's he want to do that for? Hell I don't want to see him."

Dad sighed. He studied the Kid's face for a minute, then said slowly, "Kid as sheriff of this county I got some questions to ask."

"Well now ain't that something," said the Kid.

Dad's face grew serious. The Kid said, "Now Dad there's no cause to get downright gloomy on me."

Dad stared at him and asked, "You got a will made?"

The Kid roared with laughter.

Dad said, "If you haven't got one do you want to make one?"

The Kid pointed at him and threw his head back and laughed until his face was purple.

"All right," said Dad, grinning. "Any letters you want to write?"

The Kid just smiled.

"Any last instructions? Last wishes?"

"No."

"Anything you got to say to me?"

"You don't really want me to say it now do you Dad?"

"Well you better say it before Saturday."

"I'm not hung yet."

"You will be."

"There's always that one chance in a million."

"Not this time. It's too late."

"It's never too late," smiled the Kid. "You ought to know that."

The afternoon was slipping away, the way the morning had. He lay down and fell asleep but was awakened by the slamming of the door in the room next to his. He had been wondering for some time what that room was used for and had noticed that Lon always went into it before going to Charley's. He would go in there and then there would be a heavy clump and he would leave, sometimes fussing with something or cursing. The Kid had taken to watching him as he walked over to Charley's and he noticed that Lon never carried his shotgun there. It was the shotgun, he thought, that he parked in the room next door. Could that room be the gunroom?

He heard Lon cursing now but could not make out what he was saying. And then it occurred to him that there was something wrong with the lock. He heard footsteps mounting the stairs. Lon whispered, "Why don't we get this damn lock fixed? One good shove and that door'll fly open."

"What's eating you?" Dad said. "Who's going to shove it? What you afraid of?"

"Me I'm not afraid of nothing."

"I said we'd have it fixed didn't I?"

"Forget it," Lon said.

They walked down the corridor and down the stairs. A little later the Kid and Pablo played poker. The Kid deliberately lost a few hands.

"That's a nice gun you got," he said.

Pablo stopped playing to gaze at him. "Now don't you get any ideas."

"Me? Anyway I don't want to see you get hurt. I promised your wife I'd take care of you."

Pablo laughed. "A lot you care about me Kid."

"I like you Pablo," said the Kid, smiling.

"Yeh. And you'd kill me if you thought it would do you any good."

"You know where I'll be on Monday?"

"Where?"

"You know Arroyo Grande? Below San Luis?"

"Oh yeah? And where will I be?"

"Right here. Wondering what happened."

The Kid laughed and Pablo joined him.

After a silence Pablo said, "Well...you had yourself a time. I don't reckon you got any kick coming. But it's too bad. And for killing that Johnson. They ought to give you a medal for that. You should have died an old man hombre. That way they could never say they hung you."

"That what they'll say?"

"What else?" Pablo shrugged.

"How they feel about my hanging?"

Pablo laughed.

"They're not all sorry Kid. Some say you're bad for this country. That it's time it grew up. And that with hombres like you around it's... not so good. The anglos talk like that. My people... they say you were good to them. They say stay away from the hanging Saturday morning. No good for a greaser to be seen at that party. Stay away and let the anglos know how we feel about it. About everything, now and all the way back. I'm sorry you're taking off this way."

"Why don't you help me get out of here?"

"No. We have to live with them. What we have in our heart—that's one thing. We like this country. We want to stay. It's my job. I got Maria Jesús and the boys to think about."

"And yourself."

"Sure."

"What would you do if I made a break for it?"

"I don't like it when you ask questions like that."

"You're a good boy Pablo. Remember: if the time comes— don't be a fool and get yourself killed."

"Don't worry. I got a lot of living to do."

"Me too."

"No not you. That's what I'm sorry about. Some are afraid you'll escape. Anglos mainly. Afraid what you'll do. They shouldn't have a damn greaser guarding you. That's what they say. You can never trust greasers. This greaser Pablo is going to help the Kid escape. They say, What are we waiting for? What good will it do to keep him on ice like that? They say Dad was your pard, he's going to help you escape and I'm going to help you and the only good one is Lon and they ought to kill you now."

"Good."

"What?"

"They're scared."

"You like that? I bet you do. But it's not so good for me and my people."

"Stop worrying. I'm going to be hung on the fourth. Everything will be all right for you and your people."

After dinner the afternoon went quickly. When the evening came he lit the oil lamp and later played poker with Pablo and Dad, Lon watching in the doorway. Pablo had brought in another chair. During the evening Pablo said,

"Before I was just a greaser with a badge. Now when I go out people look. This is the fellow that's guarding the Kid. Be nice to this greaser boy."

"You like them to look at you?" asked Dad.

"Sure. What about you Kid?"

The Kid shrugged and studied his cards.

"No I like it," said Pablo. "Now when I go out people stop me who never used to see me and say, What's the news of the Kid? They ask my wife and even my brother-in-law."

Lon snickered.

"What's so funny?" asked Dad, turning to look at him.

Lon shrugged and grinned.

"What you believe in Pablo?" asked Dad.

"Me? I believe in God. The Church. That I'm only a little man."

"You're not so little."

"Sure. Even in the other things I am."

"What you want to believe that for? You're not down in old Mex."

"No you believe what you believe even when they don't force you. What do you believe in Kid?"

"Nothing."

"You got to believe in something."

"I must have lost it then," the Kid said.

Pablo shook his head wonderingly. "What you believe in Dad?"

"Hell what everybody else believes in I reckon."

"You don't believe what Pablo believes," said the Kid.

"I mean us americanos."

"Sure and what do we believe in?" asked the Kid.

"God I reckon and that we're all free."

"Well now I'm not."

"I reckon not," grinned Dad.

"About God. I hear He's fast but I'd like to see for myself," said the Kid.

"You will."

The Kid laughed. "It's like burning a candle."

"Have it your way."

"What do you believe in Lon?" asked Pablo.

"Bullshit."

"Just like Lon," said Dad. "Always got to have a minority opinion on everything."

"He asked me."

"Yeh. That was *his* mistake."

Soon afterward the Kid said he was sleepy and the game broke up. As they were standing around the room the Kid said, "Dad. How about letting me wash up? My feet."

Dad eyed him skeptically. "All right."

They removed his irons and let him wash, their hands on their gunbutts. Then they locked them on him again.

"Thanks," the Kid said, smiling with pleasure. As they left the room he said, "You fellows are doing a good job. You could hang God Himself the way you're handling this."

He turned out the lamp and lay down on the bunk fully dressed. Another day gone. The moonlight was strong in the room. He fell asleep, lying on his back as he was, and did not stir much during the night.

He awoke at about six, rubbed his eyes absently, stood up, looked around the room, then remembered it was Wednesday and that on Saturday morning he was going to be hung. He went to the plaza window. The plaza was still. Smoke coming up from some of the adobes. Some riders the other side of Calle de Estrada. The jail still too: not even the sound of snoring. For the farmers the day had already begun and down at the bay it had probably begun two hours ago. He wished he could see the bay and sandhills but they were on the left and he could not get a view of them from his cell.

He went to the little chest and washed and shaved, then lay down on the bunk. Holding the leg irons taut, he slowly raised and lowered his legs about twenty times, after which he rocked back and forth. Then, holding his legs still, he swung his arms in arcs from his groin to a point over his head. He began to sweat. He went to the window again. Out there, in the middle of the plaza, was where they planned to hang him Saturday at nine o'clock. Well he did not have much time to find that one in a million.

Pablo came out of the front door and headed for Charley's, without looking up, going in that swinging tight-hipped walk of his, his gun hanging low.

One thing sure: his best chance for a break was when Lon was over in Charley's with the other prisoners. Maybe there would come a time when both Lon and Dad would be away from the jail. Lon lived in an adobe in town with his two brothers but now he was spending his nights in the jail and was almost as much a prisoner as he himself. In the room across the corridor from the gunroom were some sleeping quarters and that was where Lon and Dad slept. As for Pablo, he went home every night.

He saw Pablo returning across the plaza, carrying a board with his breakfast on it. Looking up, Pablo saw him at the window and waved. Balancing the board with one hand, he said, "Hi Kid how goes it this morning?"

"It's a good morning."

"For me it is but not for you," said Pablo, laughing, and the Kid pretended surprise.

"What do you mean by that hombre?" he asked and they both laughed.

He heard Pablo climbing the stairs and there were other footsteps also, probably Lon's, and then there was a rap on his door, the thrust of the key, a sudden pushing open of the door inward, the sight of Pablo with his drawn forty-five, the sight of Lon behind him, the English shotgun in the crook of his arm, the brief disappearance of Pablo while Lon stood in the corridor, eyeing him in hate, the clatter of dishes and Pablo bringing the breakfast in on an old coffee-stained board.

The Kid sat down on the bunk and tried the coffee. "This coffee is great Pablo, piping hot," he said sarcastically. Pablo shrugged.

It was always Pablo who went down to One-eyed Charley's for the Kid's meals. Lon had said he wouldn't wait on him if they paid him a thousand dollars to do it. Pablo sat down on the chair while Lon stood in the open doorway. After a while Pablo said, "You're not talking much today."

"That's right," the Kid said and Pablo went out and they locked him in. He lay down on the bunk and fell asleep.

When he awoke he went to the door and rapped. "Hombre!" He heard the scraping of a chair and then the shuffling of steps, then the click of the lock, and the door opened and Pablo stood in the doorway, covering it with his forty-five.

"It's too quiet," the Kid said. "How about some poker?"

"Good," said Pablo. He locked the door behind him and thrust the key into his pocket. Then they sat down and played with Pablo's deck, the Kid sitting on the bunk and Pablo taking the room's only chair. Again the Kid let Pablo win. This time Pablo was beginning to get excited.

At eleven they brought him his lunch. From twelve-thirty to two-thirty he slept again, it being siesta time. When he awoke and got up to stretch he felt as always that there was something wrong with his right thigh and he knew that the feeling was due to his gun not being strapped on it. The gun was heavy and the thigh muscles did not know how to behave yet without it. When he moved about his right leg thrust itself forward more than necessary, as if the gun was still there, and it made him uneasy because the thigh seemed uneasy, and because he was not used to being without a gun for so long.

He went to the window and saw some kids and grown-ups on the plaza, looking up. He wondered where Nika was and why she hadn't come to see him. Looking out at the people there, he wondered how it would be when the hemp was fixed around his neck. This was not how he had expected to call the turn. There was no problem dying with a gun in your hand, shooting it out, maybe killing someone, having the ball tear into you, dropping you, making you gasp with the suddenness and power of it but giving you enough time to take off like a man, maybe saying to somebody you liked, "Well I'll see you boy. So long."

When they put the hemp around his neck and jerked how

long would it take for him to choke to death? What would his legs be doing? How would his face look? Would it turn purple and look like a dried prune, making the kids laugh? Would he piss in his pants and be buried with the piss stinking on him?

He rolled a cigarette and saw that his hands were shaking. He had to steady them to light it. He had been drinking heavily the past year or so, not the region wines but raw whiskey, colored by coffee and flavored with red pepper to give it bite on the way down, and he was not the boy he had once been. His nerves had changed quite a bit.

What if his chance never came? They would say, When it came to a showdown the Kid had no sight on his gun. They would say, Hell a little adobe like that would never have kept a good man in. It sure looked as though he had been dealt a bad hand and that he was going to drop out of the game. Where was that one chance in a million? Would it come?

And then, as he took a deep drag on the cigarette, it was as though he were not standing at the window with the people watching him, as though he were not in the room at all but out in the back yard, coming out of the outhouse and running into the house and up the stairs and ramming his shoulder against the gunroom door, and he knew in a flash what his chance was and knew exactly what he must do and knew he would do it tomorrow around noon while Lon was at Charley's and he was glad he would make his play. He began to laugh, his face turning very red, and the people on the plaza watched him and glanced at each other, wondering if he had gone loco.

After dinner he and Pablo played monte. When Pablo said, "Well Kid how are you feeling now? Your time's running out," the Kid smiled that strange smile of his, the muscles bunching up around his mouth and his upper lip looking blistered underneath, and said, "I tell you Pablo it's like this. I'm feeling very good. Maybe it's your time that's running out." And he laughed as if he had heard a great joke. Pablo laughed too.

"What you think Kid? You got a chance?" asked Pablo.

The Kid made a mouth and said nothing.

As they played he thought: 'Through the back door, through the office, up the stairs to the gunroom door.' The back door swung inward. That was good. As he ran inside he would swing it shut behind him. The other door would be on his left as he came to it. It would be up against the corner, with maybe a chair in front of it. He must be sure, on the way to the outhouse, to note what had to be done there. Perhaps it was not worth fooling with that door. He would have to back out of the room with the knob in his hands and he did not have that kind of time and yet it would be well to have it shut when Pablo reached it, otherwise Pablo, who was fast, might get in a shot in the corridor just as he, the Kid, was reaching the stairhead. He would run up to the knob, grab it with both hands, then yank the door as he backed out. He must remember not to catch the shackles on the knob. And he must look out for a bulging of planks, some old knot in the wood of the floor, or some small thing, anything that might catch his heel and trip him. That second door was a problem and he must go over the action many times in his mind to prepare for it.

The important thing was to do everything slowly to be sure there were no mistakes. It was up to Pablo and Lon to make the mistakes. After all he had nothing to lose but they did and it was they who would rush into things. The front door would be open as usual but there would be no point in running onto the plaza, unless he wanted to get riddled by Lon.

After that there were the stairs—fourteen of them. What did anybody want to build stairs that steep for? A cow-hand going down there could break his neck with his high heels. They were good stairs, though, solid planks, and had a banister. He had tried it several times, pretending he had to support himself on it because of his irons, and it had felt strong enough. Fourteen stairs. He knew that by gripping the banister and flinging himself up he could vault the first four in one motion. He could do five and probably six but four were enough. One more leap and he would have done eight, and after that there were two threes and he was at the top and racing for the gunroom door. Grip, vault, pause. The pauses were important and he must forget about Pablo and Pablo's gun. Pablo had nothing to do with it.

And after that there was the lock. If the lock didn't give then things would take care of themselves. But if it gave then it was up to him to know what to do. They were damn fools not to have shot him in the back and gotten it over with. Lon was right. If you were going to kill a fellow it was no good playing with him, because the first thing you knew he might turn around and kill you first. He had gotten just one glimpse inside that gunroom but it was enough. He had been coming back with Pablo from the outhouse and had seen Lon fussing in there with something, the door wide open. Lon had seen him and said and done nothing and Pablo had said and done nothing too. It was funny how people, who usually claimed they took good care of their lives and put a pretty high price on them, got careless about the crucial things.

What he had seen had whetted his appetite. Two fairly long and dusty brown tables, with guns and ammunition scattered on them and with gunbelts hanging from nails in the walls and rifles standing in corners, dusty, or set up on the walls, and shotguns here and there. All that junk for a motheaten town and a banged-up rusty county. The ends of the tables faced the door and there was an aisle between them. Very handy to step in and select what you wanted. And on the right of the door was where Lon probably parked his shotgun when he went over to Charley's. He must remember that shotgun. Just two tables and some guns. And beyond the tables two windows, very dusty, and a couple of the panes gone and one of them badly splintered. One of the windows was close to his own cell. The other, the left one, was near the corner of the building. It would be a good place to get a bead on Lon from, dusty, the light pouring in on it, and commanding a view of the whole plaza and of Charley's. What he wouldn't give to be able to do it.

He thought: When you get to that gunroom door ram your side against it. And if it doesn't open do it again. Keep doing it even if you hear Pablo coming up to you. Keep doing it even if he shoves his gun into your back. Let him shoot, it will make no difference. But he won't shoot. He'll probably let you have it over the head with the butt. They're aiming to hang you in this town on the fourth and not to let you go out with a hot bullet. But if the door opens leave it open. If you close it behind you he can ambush you or pin you down inside. You've got to surprise him, give him no time to think, get the drop on him and disarm him. That will give you your chance. With him as a shield you're on your way. And whatever you do be sure to take your time in picking a gun. Get a good one and be sure it's loaded. Remember, take plenty of time. Because once you've got that door open you've got the town at your feet and so there's nothing to hurry about after that.

The rest of Wednesday passed quietly. When he was alone he exercised or lay on the bunk thinking of all the details on which his life would depend tomorrow, going over them until he felt he had actually lived them. Nika did not show up but he did not think much of her. If he succeeded tomorrow he would see her. When he lay down to sleep, sleep did not come. 'That's stupid,' he thought and he went to the plaza window and looked at the night-covered town. Then he went over to the chamber pot and urinated. He had been urinating often this afternoon. He lay down on his back with the determination to fall asleep and, thinking what a nice fellow Pablo was and hoping that he would not have to kill him, he fell asleep and slept deeply all night, dreaming only once—a confused dream involving Nika and some people on the plaza and a fellow he had known back in Arizona territory.

5

The next morning passed the way the others had, except that Dedrick came in on him while he was exercising and said loudly, "What you think you're doing?" holding the shotgun ready.

"Exercising," said the Kid mildly, sitting up.

"What for?"

Dad came in. "What's up?"

"He's exercising," said Lon angrily. "How about that?"

"What for Kid?" Dad asked.

"Feels good."

"Make him quit," said Lon.

"Hell do it if you want to," said Dad, walking away.

"I don't think it's right," said Dedrick.

"It's very important what you don't think," Dad said and went away.

"I'm going to be the first that throws dirt on you, so help me," said Lon passionately.

"If you live that long," smiled the Kid.

Pablo came in and watched.

Dedrick drew a rough line across the floor with his heel

and said, "That's the dead line brother. You cross that and I'll let you have it," and he held the shotgun loosely hip-high, aiming it as usual at the Kid's stomach. Glancing at Pablo, the Kid saw the dark eyes shining above the fine nose. Pablo's right hand was poised loosely above his scabbard.

The shotgun was ready, the wads were split, the hammers cocked. Lon had called the turn. His eyes were half veiled by lashes and his hands showed white with tension. The Kid looked at the two barrels staring at him, ready to rip him to shreds, and again he glanced at Pablo.

"You're a fourflusher," he said dryly and placed his right foot across the line and laughed that strange laugh of his.

Lon's tan face went a little yellow. He sucked in air.

"Hell," he said, "I'd rather see you hang." He turned and, with the shotgun in the crook of his arm, walked out of the room. But he came back immediately and pressed the muzzle of the gun against the Kid's stomach, saying, "Go ahead, why don't you make a break for it?" And he played with the triggers, the hammers cocked.

The Kid looked down at the gun, took the barrel in his small hand and pushed it aside.

"Look out that thing doesn't go off," he said.

Lon, beside himself, shoved the gun into the Kid's stomach and the Kid doubled over, gasping.

The Kid straightened up and said softly, "I'm going to get you Lon."

Lon laughed and left the room.

*

The Kid had his lunch and then Lon went to Charley's with the other prisoners. The Kid, wondering where Dad was, went to the outhouse, meaning to make his play. When he came out of the outhouse he raised his hands for the irons, glancing into Pablo's eyes. But the eyes said nothing to him. Pablo shackled him and the Kid started walking toward the adobe.

"Now's the time," he thought. But he kept thinking of Pablo's eyes and of how he had seen nothing in them, which was unlike Pablo. And then he knew that if he made his play he would not live to reach the corridor. Pablo would not hesitate. He would draw fast, shoot straight and to kill. And the Kid knew this so surely that he walked into the adobe and up the stairs and into his cell.

He would have to make his play tomorrow then or not at all. He must be cold in his mind tomorrow and around his heart he must be dead. Cold the way he was cold when someone had the drop on him. Yet he must not freeze up so that his muscles were slow. He hoped Pablo would be sensible when the time came.

That afternoon, between siesta and dinner, Lon let himself into the Kid's cell and said, "Start exercising," holding the shotgun in front of him.

The Kid smiled and said nothing.

Lon walked to the fireplace near the door, set down the shotgun and whipped out a sixgun with his left hand. Walking over to the Kid, he hit him in the face with his fist. The Kid staggered and went into a crouch. Lon hit him again, in the shoulder, and then again in the face. Blood appeared on the Kid's mouth and on Lon's hand. The Kid ran his fingers across his mouth, looking at the blood, and smiled.

"I'll be seeing you," said Lon, leaving.

"Well now I guess you will at that," said the Kid softly.

The rest of the day passed quietly and the night passed quietly too.

Next morning after breakfast a team drove up and delivered some fresh-cut lumber from the lumberyard down near the Customs House. The Kid saw the parked team from the plaza window. Lon came in and, seeing him looking out, said, "You know what that's for don't you?" Even Dad came in and said, "How do you like the new wood Kid?" The Kid smiled and said nothing. Dad said he had to ride over to Salinas but would be back that night. Lon wanted to know where he wanted the wood. Dad said out on the plaza—the carpenters would be needing it that afternoon.

That was the morning of the third, a hot drowsy morning, with a thin fog which neither cooled the town off nor let the sun through. The fog made the air hot and clammy and half the town was still sleepy. Lon went out to deal with the load of lumber and the Kid and Pablo took to playing cards. They played draw poker and the Kid kept losing steadily, winning only a hand now and then and with poor pots. Pablo offered to play stud but the Kid said draw would do. Pablo, although sleepy, was excited. And then the Kid bet his forty-four and Pablo's luck held good.

"I'll tell Dad you won it," said the Kid.

"The cards are speaking to me today."

"Yesterday too."

"Today better."

"It's not in the cards for me," said the Kid. He had been deliberately losing to Pablo.

Time passed and the Kid had his lunch and then Lon took the other prisoners to Charley's. The Kid could hear the talking downstairs, the shuffling, then Lon's voice saying up the stairway, "I'm taking them to One-eye's."

"I got you," Pablo said.

"Keep a good eye on that bastard."

"Right."

"I'm going to see him hung tomorrow morning."

Pablo winked at the Kid and said, "Take your time. It's hot today."

"Hot as shit," said Lon and he and the prisoners shuffled out of the jail. While Pablo dealt the cards the Kid rose casually and glanced out of the window. He saw Lon and the prisoners enter Charley's place.

Pablo was thinking, It's a shame he's got to hang. A nice kid. But he's not a kid any longer. They'd better stop calling him Kid. Well he won't get any older than tomorrow, that's a sure thing. The cards have been speaking to me today. When the cards speak to you there's nothing can stop you. I wonder what it's like down in Ensenada now.

And he thought of Ensenada in old Mexico, where he had been born and raised, and remembered the wide dirt streets, the sick dogs lounging in the shade, the bay, the fishing, the smell of cooking in the shacks, the hills outside of town, barren, dusty, the horsemen, the women in their cotton dresses, the long way over the mountains to Tijuana, the sand dunes, the lonely beaches, the shacks now and then.

I've come a long way, he thought. Me a poor Mexican kid. The cards are speaking to me today. Pablo you got yourself a winning streak. Don't change your luck boy.

"Hombre it looks as if I'm finished," said the Kid.

Pablo glanced at him. "Sorry hombre."

"So am I."

"What a life," said Pablo.

"Better than hanging," said the Kid. He shrugged. "I think I'll go to the outhouse."

"Sure," Pablo said.

The Kid preceded him to the outhouse. While he was inside Pablo stood in the hot yard, his gun out of its scabbard, casually pointing at the half-open door. When the Kid came out Pablo clamped the shackles on his wrists and they returned to the house. Then, near the door, the Kid tripped and stumbled and half ran and half fell into the house and before Pablo realized it he was out of sight. But Pablo was not frightened, for where could the Kid go and what could he shoot with? Maybe it was a little joke. Still, he Pablo would have to stop it.

He jerked his gun and ran toward the door. Just before he made it he tripped, just as the Kid had done, and almost fell on his face. While he was on his hands and knees he remembered the broken lock on the gunroom door and then he was frightened, for what if the Kid knew that a good push would fling the door open? What if the Kid was making for it now and had in mind to grab a gun? The Kid with a gun was a terrible thing. He could shoot your eye out at many paces. Almost any gun, he knew them all, they spoke to him.

He fumbled with the door, his hands trembling, and ran through the little office, thinking as he ran: Maybe he's not after the gunroom at all. Maybe he'll run out the front door onto the plaza. But there's nothing out there but all that sun and we'll shoot him down like a dog. Then he fumbled with the other door and heard the Kid clanking up the stairs and he thought, He's shackled, I'll catch him before he gets to the top. What have I got to be worried about? Only damn him I ought to kill him for doing this to me. And then he heard the Kid fling himself against the gunroom door and he went cold from his groin to his feet, running as he was down the corridor to the stairhead.

Get out of here, he thought. His legs wanted to run back into the yard. Run out and call Lon. That slob, eating. Burn the house down. Riddle it. No you stay out of this. You know what Maria Jesús will say. White man's business. Know what's good for you Pablo. You're only a greaser and don't forget it. Get out of this pronto. If you get yourself killed what will Maria Jesús care about the reasons?

Then he thought: But how did he know about that door? A thing like that can get me killed. I told Lon we ought to fix that lock and he said, What for? What the hell for? I told Dad about it and he said, Sure we'll get a man up here one of these days to take care of it. Damn them they ought to know it's bad luck to let a lock run down like that. And then he heard the Kid throw his weight against the door a second time and he thought he heard the door fly open. If the Kid made a getaway he Pablo was through in this town. How could he explain to Maria Jesús? And to his kids when they grew up? He had better run up those stairs and stop the Kid before there was any trouble. It was better to stop him before Lon over in Charley's knew anything had happened. It was better to stop it now and keep it a secret that it had ever happened at all.

At the head of the stairs he met the Kid. The Kid was just coming out of the gunroom, a forty-five in his right hand.

"Drop it," he said.

Pablo was paralyzed. He was not really aiming his gun.

He could not make his arm move. But the Kid was aiming well. Pablo could see the muzzle pointing at his stomach. He could see the Kid clearly—the small blond head, the slate-colored eyes, the invisible lashes, the pinched white nose, the strong small hands, the small feet, the black trousers, the soft white shirt and the smile around the purplish lips.

"Drop it Pablo," the Kid said softly.

But Pablo could neither raise the gun nor drop it. Then he remembered his streak of good luck, how the cards were speaking to him today and how he, a greaser, was a trusted deputy in this town, and he thought of the new-cut wood and of how he had won the Kid's forty-four and he remembered Maria Jesús and the kids and he whirled at the stairhead and ran down the stairs, taking them two at a time, careful however not to fall, meaning to get around the corner and wing the Kid from there.

"Hombre!" cried the Kid.

Then Pablo went flying and he thought he had tripped. His face struck the stairs and his legs windmilled in a clatter and he fell into the vestibule and against the jamb of the front door, striking the jamb so hard that the Kid felt the vibration in the stairway. He lay with the small of his back against the jamb, his head and shoulders outside, the sunlight brilliant on his dark skin and white shirt. His black hair looked rich and thick and his ears were clean and small, but for the rest his head was bloody. Blood was running from his nose and mouth and had covered his black mustache. His eyes looked into the sun without blinking. The Kid turned to go about his business.

Then Pablo heard the shot and he knew the ball had hit him. He tried to rise but couldn't, there were chains and shackles on him, pinioning his arms and legs, and great weights holding him down. There was no pain but he knew he was dying and he wanted to get outside to die out there. So he got to his hands and knees and, like a blind bear, crawled and scuttled on to the grass, saying nothing, not even groaning, not even feeling the hot flow of blood across his chest, hardly seeing anything, and he scuttled out of there to avoid a second shot, but the second shot did not come, and he scuttled out onto the plaza which was so full of golden light. But the plaza looked as though evening had come on it and he thought it was night in Ensenada and that the fishing was good and that Maria Jesús was visiting her sister and he crawled a little way south in the direction of his house on the Calle de Estrada on the way to the mission, leaving blood on the long grass, and when he had gotten about as far as the first window it occurred to him that it ought to be morning and that there ought to be plenty of light on the plaza and he wondered if this were the plaza and why he was lying down and then suddenly he thought: They ought to use some of that lumber to make my coffin, and it seemed to him important that he tell somebody that and he tried to crawl as far south as he could, going diagonally across the plaza, and suddenly he saw the mission and the altar and the sun blinded him and, sobbing "Dios me perdone!" he died.

In the outhouse the Kid had known that this was his last chance, the one in a million. The load of lumber had convinced him of it. He was not exactly surprised to see the lumber and yet he had not thought of it in just that way. He had not thought clearly of the gallows but only of the hemp noose and the jerking and the crowds and the jeering and the possibility of urinating in his trousers. But now he knew that the gallows would be built and that this was his only chance for his life. He knew what he had to do.

When he came out he held up his hands for Pablo to shackle them and he looked into Pablo's eyes but Pablo's eyes did not want to meet his. Pablo replaced his gun in the scabbard and put the warm shackles on the Kid's wrists. This is the time, thought the Kid. Try not to fall if you get hit. It doesn't matter if I'm hit as long as I don't go down, as long as I can reach that door and come out of there with a gun in my hand. He thought: When you get to that stone before the doorway do it. He looked into Pablo's eyes again but Pablo's eyes did not meet his. I must keep looking into his eyes, he thought, I must make him wonder why I'm doing it. He lingered a little, but seeing that Pablo's eyes would not meet his he went ahead of him, carrying his shackled wrists in front of his stomach, shuffling along with his shackled ankles, and now he knew that he must not look back, must not look back even if he suspected that Pablo's gun was out and pointing. There was nothing now he could do except to forget Pablo entirely, forget Nika, forget Lon over in Charley's, forget what day it was, the heat, the drowsiness, and why he was doing this. There was only the small pleasant thing to do—to reach the small gray stone about a yard from the doorsill, sitting there like an old toad, to pretend to stumble on it, to go headlong as though in a play, to run crouching through the doorway and headlong up the stairs, never hurrying, going with care so as not to stumble. For if he stumbled he would never get another chance. There was only one, not two, in a million.

When he came to the stone he stumbled and ran into the house and up the stairs and when he reached the stairhead he ran to the door and threw his shoulder against it twice and it flew open as he had expected. He felt wonderfully lucky that he had gauged it right and he knew now that he couldn't miss, that his luck was holding up and that the whole town could not hold him that day against his will. When the door flew open he caught an image in his mind of all that fresh-cut lumber waiting and then of the new gallows waiting and he smiled and wondered what was keeping Pablo, not knowing that Pablo had stumbled just as he had pretended to stumble, as though in a necessary act of imitation.

He glanced at the hot room and saw the guns lying on the table, picked one up, spun the chambers, saw it was loaded, cocked the hammer and moved lithely into the corridor. It was just then that Pablo saw him. He could have cut Pablo down easily but he had figured on Pablo's being frightened and had decided not to shoot unless necessary, he had figured that Pablo's being frightened might save Pablo's life. But then Pablo turned and ran and then it was out of the Kid's hands. Pablo had made a mistake and now there was nothing the Kid could do. He ran down the corridor to the stairhead and saw Pablo going full tilt down the stairs and he fired before he knew it, fired without aiming, and the ball as usual knew where to go, it spoke for the Kid as they all did, hit Pablo in the back just slightly above the heart, while Pablo was in the air running and leaping, and when the Kid saw the dark spot appear on Pablo's back he did not wait to see what Pablo did, he knew that his relations with Pablo were ended and that Pablo would have no more troubles in this world, and so he turned from the stairhead and ran back into the gunroom and picked up Lon Dedrick's sweet English shotgun.

He had not figured on the cards turning up this way but now that they had it was all right with him and he knew what his next move must be. He knew Lon inside out. He knew what

Lon would do. Lon would figure on his escaping into the back yard, where the outhouse was, avoiding the open plaza, and he would come running down around the north side of the adobe to stop him, knowing he could not travel fast in his irons. That was why he waited for him in the gunroom. He could kill Lon with one of the Winchesters or even with the forty-five which had killed Pablo, but it was not in the cards, the cards said he must kill him with his own sweet English shotgun. He felt wonderful standing in the gunroom, peering out the window, waiting. This was his day and he could not miss no matter how hard he tried. It was wonderful to be waiting to kill Lon Dedrick.

He could kill him with a barrelful so that Lon would never know what hit him but that was not the way it was going to be. It was important to let Lon know who killed him and how. Otherwise the fun was gone out of it. There were many ways to kill a man but this was the sweetest. You had to let him know the truth of what happened. You had to give him that last moment of truth before you killed him.

He did not mind the shackles or the jail or the town. He knew he had won and that nothing could stop him. He was no longer a kid, he was feeling his age, and he had been loving and drinking too much for his good but he was still all right on his legs and in the quick thinking and the shot that had killed Pablo had been as good as ever and now he had won and he was going to show this town how to make a getaway and he knew that no one would try to stop him, knowing that this was his day.

It was too bad about Pablo, whom he could see lying in the sun on the plaza, lying on his face, his arms outstretched, the fingers like claws, a little blood on the gray shirt on his back. Pablo oughtn't to have run. He ought to have controlled his legs. That little lack of control could cost a man his life. That was why it was important to be ice-cold in your mind and heart when the bad moments came. Soon there was going to be a bad one for Lon Dedrick. It was going to be interesting to see how much control Lon would have.

He could see Lon running out of Charley's, the forty-five in his hand. He could imagine those thin bluish legs in Lon's trousers, carrying the paunch, and he could imagine the breasts bobbing in that run. He could see Lon's dark hair, long, flying, and the small upturned nose and the cleft chin and the open collar of his shirt, and the glint of the sun on the forty-five. He got the shotgun ready, pointing the barrel through the broken dusty pane, covering Lon all the way, ready to kill him if he swerved off but knowing that he would come close, come just under the window. Lon could not possibly see him in that room, with the dusty panes and the light so bright on the plaza.

He saw Lon's face when he caught sight of Pablo, saw it twitch with fear and saw the gun hand leap up, as if to shoot at the dead man, heard him curse and saw him scan the adobe quickly, still running. Someone cried out, "The Kid's killed Patron!" It was an old man's voice. Lon started at the sound. His luck was running out fast while the Kid's was very good that day. Another voice called out, "The Kid's killed Patron!"

But no one ventured out onto that plaza except Lon, whose job it was to come get him. Lon wasn't happy about this. His eyes showed fear and his cleft chin looked as if he had spilled milk on it. I'll bet he wishes he had this shotgun, thought the Kid.

"Hi Lon," he said mildly through the broken pane.

Lon was just below him, holding the forty-five ready. He looked up, saw the Kid's face, saw the black muzzles facing him and cried, staggering back, "He's killed me too!"

The Kid pulled the trigger of one barrel.

It had been a good meal and Lon had eaten well. Meat loaf, creamed onions, baked potato, string beans, white bread and black coffee. Lon used to say, "When I eat I got the whole world buried." He was not much of a talker when he ate. Not much of a thinker either. When he ate that meal he did not think of the Kid or Pablo or Dad or his other prisoners. Eating was a full-time occupation for Lon.

He was having his coffee when he heard the shot across the plaza. "Hell!" he cried. "That greaser's killed him!" And, knowing his other prisoners would not have the guts to escape, he drew his gun, rushed out of Charley's into the dazzling light and ran toward the jail. He thought he saw something lying to the left of the door but was not certain. And then he heard an old man's voice shout, "The Kid's killed Patron!" and he thought, "That's shit." But the peculiar stillness of the plaza stopped him. If Pablo had killed the Kid he would have come out onto the plaza and shown himself, yet the plaza was empty and the jail very still. And then, coming closer to the house, he made out Pablo lying in front of it.

Somebody shouted, "The Kid's killed Patron."

Lon was under the north upper room of the jail when he heard someone say, "Hi Lon."

He knew from that moment that he was dead and he wished with all his life that he could do it over again, the coming out of Charley's and crossing the plaza, for he knew he had made a mortal mistake. And then, glancing up to where the voice had come from, he saw the black muzzles eyeing him and he urinated in his trousers. Staggering back, he cried, "He's killed me too!"

And then the Kid pulled the trigger and the hammer came flipping down on the charge and the charge blew the nine buckshot down the long barrel and at the muzzle's end they scattered and all nine hit Lon on the left side of his stomach, shredding it, and it was like nine white-hot pokers going inside him and he screamed a long high-pitched scream and screamed again as he was falling and grabbed at his stomach and tried to scream but couldn't and fell to his knees and pitched onto his face and lay in a pool of blood, thinking he was out on the sea in a skiff in a high wind under the overhanging rocks, smelling the stink of the seawolves. Then the skiff filled with water and the water got into his lungs and, gasping for breath, he knew he was dying. And then, in a flash, he saw himself as if from a great distance, standing on the plaza on that hot bright morning, standing under the window, and saw himself get shot and the bitterness of it was that the Kid had outlived him, and he thought, I'm killed, the son of a bitch has killed me, they'll all be saying he killed me. So long you shits, you're shits all of you. Ma, you fix it like you always do. He urinated again and began to dream but the dreams were mixed up and he was too tired to straighten them out and at last, drooling blood and pumping blood from his nostrils, he stopped dreaming and it was over.

The Kid walked down the corridor, down the stairs, out onto the plaza, aimed the gun and blew part of Lon's head off with the other nine buckshot. Then he broke the gun against the ground and threw the pieces onto Lon, saying, "Here Lon here's your shotgun." And he stood there looking at him but he was not smiling. It's a fact he hated that Lon Dedrick as much as he had hated any man.

6

That was how the Kid escaped. There are some other details but they are not important —how he got the keys off Patron and unlocked his shackles; went to the gunroom and got two gunbelts and another forty-five; went down to the stable, saddled up and left that town in his dust. The plaza was as empty as a graveyard at midnight. Nobody felt like calling the Kid's hand.

He made for the Punta, where Harvey French, Bob Emory and I were lying low. We had been spending most of our time in the hills but on this Friday we had come down for the change. There was great excitement all over the place. We got bedrolls, food, guns, ammunition and a bag of gold coins we had hidden away; also a fresh horse for the Kid. We made for the wagon road. As we neared the plaza he pulled up, turning to me casually.

"Where's Nika?" he asked.

I was expecting to hear him ask that. She was not around the Punta that afternoon.

"I don't know. I haven't seen her around today," I said. He cut off toward the plaza and looked in at her adobe, then rode over to Francesca Zamora's, the old Indian woman. Francesca did not know either. She was about to tell him something but I made a motion of my hand which the Kid did not see and she did not tell him the thing which I myself would have to tell him in a day or two. As we wheeled and galloped off she cried out something which we could not make out.

The thing I knew and which everybody knew was that Nika Machado had got herself married while the Kid was in jail. I was afraid of what he might do if he found out there. I was afraid he might go in and kill Miguel Gomez and maybe kill her too. If he did we'd have a free-for-all and the chances are we would not get off the Punta alive. Miguel had asked Nika to marry him when he was sure he was dying. She had. I didn't know the particulars but I knew these facts were true. Maybe I could have smuggled the information to the Kid in the jail and maybe not, but I didn't try, seeing as how it could have done him no good and might have done him some harm. The Kid would be sore at me for holding out on him but I had no choice. We had to get going and to get going pronto. As we galloped out some of the natives waved and shouted and some stood and stared, knowing what Nika had done and wondering, probably, if the Kid knew.

As soon as we stopped to rest our horses we wanted to hear how he had escaped. We stood around him, grinning, and threw questions at him but all he said was, "You muchachos sure are nosy." He lifted a whiskey bottle to his mouth, drank, said "Kiss me baby" and passed the bottle around.

"Kiss me baby," we said and took a swig. Then he told us

the story. We sure laughed when we heard it. I just doubled up when I heard how good old Lon had taken it. That story added years to my life. We stood there swigging on a high bluff above the sea and talked about Dad and how the ranchers would hound him out of the country and how life was good for us but not so good for Lon and Pablo and Dad. Man we sure as hell laughed and slapped each other on the back. And Harvey he'd hop up and do a jig.

It was great to have the Kid back. We couldn't believe our luck. We had been waiting for him to hang and now here he was, in the flesh and raring to go. He was like a spring that's suddenly cut loose. You could see what it meant to him to be free again—the way he ate and drank, laughed, whooped, slapped us on the back, did a jig now and then, jumped on his horse, the way his eyes shone and his muscles humped. He was going to make up for lost time, I could see that.

"We ought to stick around here and shoot Dad in the ass," he said. "What do you say Harvey?"

But Harvey thought it was kind of risky at the moment.

"We'll be back," said the Kid. "We'll tree this country."

"Hell all it needs is lightning bugs and corncobs to stampede those poodles," I said.

"Tonight we'll kill ourselves a yearling and eat beef straight. How about it boys?" asked the Kid.

"It's great to have you back," Harvey said.

"What do you say we go to old Mex and have some fun?" asked the Kid.

Harvey and I liked the idea but Bob said nothing.

"What you got on your mind Bob?" asked the Kid.

"I think you ought to hide out in the hills," Bob said.

"Why? What's wrong with old Mex?"

"We can lose ourselves in the hills," Bob said. "Take good care of ourselves in there. When this thing blows over we can go south. But right now Dad'll be telegraphing to all that country below."

"You aiming to jinx me Bob?" asked the Kid.

"You know me better than that," said Bob.

"Do I?"

"Well if you don't know me by now you never will," said Bob.

We decided to go to old Mex. Later that afternoon Bob and I were riding abreast and the Kid and Harvey were riding up ahead.

Bob said, "Me jinxing him."

"Forget it," I said.

"What's got into him?"

"Forget it Bob," I said.

"It's that Nika who's jinxing him."

"His luck was never better. Forget it Bob. Forget it," I said.

It was still early afternoon when we had set out. We headed for the Rancho El Sur country, where we had often rustled cattle. It was not easy going. Up and down: even though we hugged the coast as much as we could. Up the shoulder of one golden hill and then down to a creek or a canyon; then up again, twisting, heading seaward, then inland, but always trying to strike south as nearly straight as we could. The sea was always there with us, or almost always, and it was never dead gray or dead blue but very blue or very green. When you saw it from high up it looked calm but when you saw it from beach level the heaving and the swells reminded you it was no lake you were looking at. The hills were on our left. In the hills there was plenty of game, also lion, bear and boar. We were always fording creeks and picking our way across canyons. I can remember some of the names—Wildcat, Malpaso, Joshua and Sierra creeks; Granite, Palo Colorado and Wildcat canyons. We carried field glasses with which we surveyed the country ahead, the hills and canyons and the long beaches. And we kept checking the country behind us for any signs of a posse. But we were traveling fast, our horses were fresh and we had a good start and so we did not really think the posses would catch us.

When we hit the Rancho El Sur it made us sad to pass through it without taking something. It was one of those huge ranchos where it was no trick at all to help yourself. Lots of cattle lived and died without ever seeing a man and there were no fences. We would go in and cut out what we wanted and move north again, changing brands in one of the canyons. We could dispose of our haul with no trouble, our connections in this respect being of the best.

The Kid sang a lot as we rode along. I reckon he liked that country better than any he had ever known, although to tell the truth I don't know exactly what other country he'd known. He never said much about his past and what he did say sounded as if he was kidding us. I heard it said that he was mixed up in the Lincoln County War, also in some of the Tombstone and Trinidad doings but I don't know for sure. I even heard a story once that he was born in Boston, was sent to the House of Refuge as a child and bound out to a western farmer, from whom he escaped. But it sounds like bull to me.

The first part of the trip we did not cut inland but when we thought we might be approaching settlements we did, although we knew that nobody we might meet would know what had happened, because they did not have a telegraph line running down this stretch of coast for about a hundred and fifty miles, the line going down the valley road, the old Camino Real, and hitting the coast at around San Luis Obispo—the Bishop. Still, it would look funny, the Kid's being on the loose. We figured that everybody round about would know that he was due to hang. But if we met somebody who wanted trouble we could give it to them. We were lugging a whole traveling armory. The horses were carrying a load and they knew it. We figured on getting fresh ones from friends all down the line or stealing what we needed.

We kept going all that afternoon and a good part of that night, stopping now and then to rest our horses and rousing friends to get fresh ones. We had a fair moon to light our way. A moonless trail would have been very dangerous in that terrain. As it was, we had to be careful. The way was often treacherous and full of fog. The fog drifted inland and sat over canyons, gullies and coves, showing only the tops of the highest hills and sometimes slinking far inland.

We would hit patches of it lasting half a mile and go in and out of it as if we were passing through smoke-filled rooms. It silenced everything, making the surf sound like a long-drawn sigh, our voices as thin as in a snowstorm, and the hoofbeats as if the shoes were covered with burlap. There was much to do guiding our horses, picking their way through fog and moonshadow for them. Although they were good horses and probably knew more about all this than any man could ever know, we could not take a chance at such a time and we let them only carry us, we ourselves supplying eyes, nose, ears and seventh sense. We camped out without a fire and ate our dinner cold: jerkin, whiskey and some bread. We took turns standing watch. We figured we were somewhere east of Lucia. The next night we made it to about Point Piedras Blancas and the following night to the outskirts of San Luis. And so in three days we made that lonely trip and came out near the main coast road.

The next night we camped out in a wooded place near a stream. It was so remote that we chanced a fire to have us some hot food. It was my turn to take the first watch and practically a minute after we finished eating I was the only one awake. Bob and Harvey were asleep over on the left, the horses were quietly stomping in the shadows near by, and the Kid, propped against a tree-trunk, seemed to be asleep on the right of the fire. He looked like a greaser sitting there, with his black tight trousers, black high-heeled boots, black sombrero tilted over his face, and the brown blanket covering his shoulders like a serape.

I poked at the fire, thinking that the time had come to tell him about Nika and hating to have to do it. I went over to him and crouched down beside him.

"Kid," I whispered.

After a little pause he said, "Hm?" I could not see his face because of the sombrero.

"Kid I got something to tell you."

"Hm."

"Nika got married."

He did not stir. For a second I thought he was asleep.

Then he said, "What about it?" in a bored voice.

"I thought you'd want to know."

"Who to?"

"Miguel. Miguel Gomez."

"When?"

"Wednesday."

He said nothing. I got tired of crouching and stood up. When Harvey's watch came I woke him and fell asleep almost at once. The Kid was still propped against that same pine tree.

In the mountains behind Santa Barbara we had friends. We got fresh horses and a good stock of food and we rested up for the night. Next morning very early we rode down toward the foothills and looked down at the town from a clump of pines. It looked white and peaceful in the bright sun and very green with all the trees and gardens. The sea lay blue beyond it. We sat our horses and looked at it, tired of running, tired of the back trails and the salt taste in our mouths and the dried meat and the canned goods and the stink of dried sweat on us. My left shoulder ached from holding the reins and I was beginning to feel as saddle-sore as a tenderfoot. We were getting tired of everything—even of each other's company, even of the smell of our horses.

We returned to the back trails and headed in the direction of Ventura. Harvey knew these trails pretty well and so we had to approach the main road only occasionally. It was not surprising that he knew them. Each of us knew parts of that country. We had tried to study as much of it as we could. A fellow in our business rarely studied the main roads except to know where they were. It was the back trails we wanted to know and we made a habit of learning them throughout a whole territory, the way a fellow will learn a language his life may depend on. In that way our heads got to be full of stuff that would have amazed a man in another line of business. We knew caves, gullies, shacks, shortcuts, ranchos, adobes and friends up and down that terrain, the way a river pilot would know snags, currents, islands, changing banks, depths and whatelse not, know them so well that he felt them, even in the dark. We passed behind Ventura not far from the mission and, making good time, did not quit until we were just short of Camarillo that night.

After supper the Kid and I stretched our legs a bit, with Harvey and Bob minding camp, and the Kid turned to me and asked, "Why didn't she come to see me in that calabozo?"

"She meant to," I said. "But he got sick and she nursed him. I think she was going to see you on Friday, in the afternoon."

"What was the matter with him?"

"Got kicked by a mare. Started coughing blood. Then he came down with fever. May be dead right now for all I know."

"What she marry him for?"

I shrugged. "You got me."

"She say anything to you about it?"

"Me? She kept clear of me. Only thing she said was she had no use for you. She can't forgive you for that Juanita."

"Wonder how old Dad is doing," he said.

"Yeh. Good old Dad."

"I'd give Bob's right eye to know what he's doing."

"He must be catching hell."

The Kid laughed. I glanced at him. He had changed all right but it was hard to put your finger on it. Maybe the closeness of that noose had changed him—I don't know. He was more quiet than ever and there seemed to be something eating at him behind his eyes.

On our eighth day out the Kid had a hankering, as he put it, to see some new faces and so we made our way over to a little place called El Segundo on the coast, and as luck would have it they had a baile going. We hoisted in a cargo of aguardiente and started dancing and people kept drinking toasts to the Kid's escape and after a while there were a couple of fistfights from all the good feeling and I could see the Kid was feeling great.

"Well how does it feel to be out?" I asked and slapped him on the back.

"Kiss me baby," he said and tossed down some aguardiente, then went back to dancing with a little Mexican girl he had taken a liking to. They were dancing like that when up comes this fellow named Tom Murphy, a forty-niner, and pokes her in the rear and meows. She was scared to death and jumped three feet high. The Kid caught him by the collar but the women began to scream and he let him go.

"You better beat it," said the Kid.

But the old fellow only cackled and went to the other side of the room. He had a bushy gray beard and a paunch and two bum thin legs and a little scar across one nostril and under his eye.

"He's always doing that," a fellow said. "Likes to snake up behind somebody and poke a finger up their rear."

"That's a good habit," said the Kid.

"Yeh," said the fellow. "Tried it on a cowpuncher a couple of months back and this fellow horsewhipped him on the main street."

A little while later this old coot sneaked up and goosed the Kid's girl again. This time some men led the old fellow out and the Kid just stood there with his hands in his back pockets and his small close-cropped head hunched over and watched Murphy with his cold slate-colored eyes and I knew that he wanted to see the corpse of that old bird. Sure enough, about five minutes later he excused himself and went outside, caught up with Murphy in a potato field, cracked down on him and shot him through the chest, without a word.

The ball hit Murphy on the left side and sent him spinning

as if he had been yanked backward by a reata. He landed on his hands and knees, gasping, the blood all over his back, a great look of surprise on his face, and he looked down at his chest and looked at the Kid, his face white as death, and saw the Kid smiling at him, and he tried to get up to explain something, probably that the Kid had made a mistake, and then something hit him and his eyes clouded over and he fell in a heap in the mud of the potato field.

I had followed the Kid outside.

"Let's get going," said the Kid. "That fellow has spoiled my fun."

But before we left El Segundo we went down to the ocean for a swim and the Kid's mood improved. We shouted and whooped and dived off the rocks, having a hell of a time. We lay on the rocks in the moonlight, then slowly dressed and strapped on our belts. While Harvey and Bob and I sat around, the Kid practiced drawing.

"About time you did that," I said.

"He doesn't need it," said Harvey.

"Everybody needs it," the Kid said.

"They had you cooped up a long time," said Bob.

"Never again," said the Kid.

You thought he was kind of dreaming the way he stood there, his legs spread a little and his body hunched over, his toes turned in, he looking out toward the ocean, his right hand meanwhile going through the motions of the draw. He didn't wear his scabbard slung low, like the rest of us. He said a low scabbard made you reach and wasted time. He would raise his hand about as high as his head and bring it down and just touch the gunbutt, getting his last three fingers under it, his trigger finger pointing straight out and the thumb standing straight up and ready. He would do that over and over again. Then he would hold his hand down by his side and do the same thing. He would practice getting his last three fingers under the butt from various parts of his body, sometimes looking down at the butt and at other times just feeling where it was. He didn't bother to draw the gun out of its scabbard.

Of course he sometimes did draw the gun and sometimes he drew both of them but when he was in action he never used both at the same time. I've never known a good gunfighter stupid enough to try to fight with two guns at the same time, or one who did and lived long enough afterward to write home about it, if he had a home and if he could write. Fact is it takes only one bullet to kill a man and one gun to send the bullet home and if you mess around with two guns, even if you can shoot pretty well with your left hand as well as your right, you're going to have your grave dug for you. Those stories about the Kid shooting in two directions at the same time and bringing down both men were made up by boys who were great fighters with their pencils. The Kid used to laugh at such stories.

I don't mean to say that fellows wouldn't draw two guns. They would, but the good ones shot only one at a time, using the second for a spare and to prove they had reserve power, especially if they were facing a mob. When the first gun went empty they could make the border shift faster than your eye could spot it and then the second gun would come into play, but not before then. That way they shot cool and straight, which is why they stayed alive.

Same thing with gunfanning. You've probably heard of Smoky Hill Clifton, a great gunfanner in his day—great in exhibition matches. He had no trigger on his guns and could make them pour lead in a stream. One day he and the Kid had words and Smoky Hill, who had only heard of the Kid but had never seen him operate, asked the Kid to come outside (they were in a saloon in Salinas) and exchange the compliments of the season.

"Glad to oblige," said the Kid, smiling.

They went out into the street, Smoky Hill going out first and walking a way south, and then they started coming toward each other. Fellows were saying that the Kid didn't stand a chance against this kind of fighter. Smoky Hill was a tall Texas man and he came down the street tall and cool-looking, wearing spurs that clanked. He started shooting first and before you knew it his gun was empty. The Kid kept coming, without drawing his gun. Then he stopped and I thought sure he had been hit. His right hand was hanging at his side and then, before you knew he had tried to draw, the forty-four was in his hand and he took aim and fired one shot which hit Smoky Hill in the heart and that was the end of that shooting match. Two of Smoky Hill's shots had hit the Kid, one grazing his left shoulder and the second his left thigh, but it was Smoky Hill who was lying there dead. His gunfanning hadn't helped him a hell of a lot.

I got tired of just sitting there watching the Kid practice and so I stood up and practiced too, yanking my sixshooter every time, until I could feel the hard tightness in the front of my shoulder. It was good to feel the gun fly up into my hand. As soon as I began to practice the Kid turned his back on me and climbed behind a ledge out of view. I was used to that and I didn't mind. He didn't like to see a man draw, no matter who it was. Well we all have our peculiarities, that's for sure.

We sensed the change of climate clearly. The sea winds became softer, the fog got thinner until there was almost none of it and the ocean looked softer and bluer on the occasions when we came out of the hills and saw it. The trees thinned out and changed, the pines giving way to eucalyptuses, chestnuts and olives, and the mountains and hills did not seem as rugged as those of the Santa Lucias which we had left behind. But meanwhile we were fagging out, losing fat fast and feeling it and in need of sugar and red meat all the time. We had stubbles and looked haggard and our eyes were shot from the dust and lack of sleep and the brilliant light. It was not doing our tempers any good.

The Kid and Bob kept having words. I don't think the Kid ever liked Bob much. Bob was a big fellow, tall and heavy, light-haired, with a ruddy face, and he weighed more than two hundred pounds, probably. The Kid had no love lost for that size of fellow. Bob ate like a horse and young as he was had a paunch and was a great farter. The Kid didn't take to that free and easy farting. He was very neat and gentlemanly in his

manners and would never have done a thing like that in anybody's company. But Bob did it because it seemed natural to
him and because he thought it was funny and he was not too
neat about his eating and clothes. But he was easy to get along
with and there were some of us who were a lot less delicate
than he was. It was Bob, you will remember, who came for
my horses the first time I met the Kid and who backed down
when I outdrew him. We got along all right after that. But I
had a hunch even then the Kid didn't like him and I was pretty
sure of it when he asked Bob to cook for us then, to cook for
me too, and I being a stranger to the bunch.

When the Kid and I were alone I told him that while it was
none of my business I hoped it was not serious between him
and Bob because it was not good to think there was trouble
among us. He said I had it all wrong, that there was no
trouble at all, and I could see by that that he did not like my
mixing in and so I dropped the matter. My own temper was
pretty bad. We had taken to riding all day without as much as
twenty words except at mealtimes. But what can you expect
when you ride together day in day out, morning noon and
night? Even Harvey had times when he was glum but for the
most part he sure fooled me. I had never thought he would take
that kind of grind in good humor but he did. I'll be damned to
this day if I can make out what he had to be laughing about.
He was always grinning, making jokes, doing jigs and acting
as if he was drunk. I had never seen him like that. I wonder if
he had a hunch he was going to die soon. I have been around
a number of fellows that have taken off, old and young,

and have noticed that sometimes they have this hunch, although they usually aren't aware of it. They themselves are not aware of it but a fellow who knows them is and is puzzled by it. Then when you have seen them take off you understand what it meant.

What did Harvey have to be laughing about? I did not understand what the big joke was about and he got on my nerves with all that glad face and we had some words ourselves. But the Kid never said an unpleasant word to Harvey. He was saving them all for Bob. There would be nothing ugly but it would have been better if there had. We'd be riding along a mountain trail, single file or maybe two abreast, and the Kid would say thinly, with a dry smile,

"I wish you wouldn't pull up short like that Bob."

I'd look around to see what was up and so would Harvey, for it was not like Bob to pull up short unless he had to. Then Bob would say, "What do you mean Kid?" and there would be that whiteness around his lips.

"Just don't pull up short," the Kid would say evenly and Bob would say,

"I didn't," and the Kid would say,

"You're wrong Bob you did. I wish you wouldn't do it again," and Bob would reply, trying to control his voice.

"What are you getting at Kid?"

"Nothing."

"Why don't you tell me what it's about?"

"Just don't pull up short."

"All right," Bob would say, seeing it was useless to argue.

And then we'd have hours of silence from everybody, until the next little incident. Meanwhile Harvey would break out into singing now and then. I wondered if he had gone loco. As for the Kid, it seemed to me that he should have been in good spirits, having made his great escape. I know I would have been if I were in his boots. But I wasn't in his boots and that's a fact, isn't it? Now if you'd have come to me after I made a great escape like that and said, "Doc is there anything eating you?" I would have said, "Bob somebody's got to do a little work on your noodle—a major operation I guess."

Once I went off to a stream to wash and when I came back to our camp I saw the Kid poke a forefinger against Bob's chest and say, "Bob I wouldn't keep talking like that if I was you."

"Why? What'd I say?"

"I'm just telling you."

Bob looked amazed and even though I didn't know what it was about I couldn't blame him. What was eating the Kid? Bob should have lit out then and there. Anyhow that was how it began and you know the consequence, how the Kid killed Bob and how that killing affected him more than any other killing of his life. The Kid was sure acting peculiar, as if his attention was hundreds of miles away, as if he had something important to tend to, somebody important to see and set things straight with. I had never seen him like that.

We were very tired now and believe me mister it's not my habit to exaggerate. You stay on a horse all that time, pushing hard every day and part of the night when you can, and after a while you've got no legs, bottom or arms and you don't care, except that you've still got that jumpy spine, which never stops expecting a bullet to come out of somebody's Sharps gun a long way off and cut you in two. We didn't know what we were letting ourselves in for, heading for the border all in one swallow. To hear some folks tell of our ride you'd think it was a Sunday-afternoon trot. All I know is, young as we were it pretty near knocked hell out of us. Santa Monica, San Juan Capistrano, Encinitas—we hit the outskirts of them all, laying out at night. And then, on the thirteenth, we crossed the border outside of Tijuana and knew we had made it. They had border guards on the outlook for us but we had friends who had heard of our coming and we slipped across at night in their company. Luckily there was no moon.

Tijuana in those days was just a sleepy border town and not the small-time Coney Island it is now: no night clubs for the gringos, no fast divorce mills, and no kohinoors sold on the main streets. It was smaller, quieter and just as dirty but there were some good haciendas around and not half the scum you find now, from both sides of the border. We stayed clear of the town and lay out in a small hacienda about eight miles south, where we had friends, and where we took our time resting up, but we came into town in the evenings and you would have thought the Kid was a conquering general the fuss the greasers made over him. The news of his great escape had of course spread even down there.

We played faro and monte but without luck. The Kid had always been lucky at cards but the Mexican air didn't do him any good. Once, while he was losing, he said to me out of the corner of his mouth:

"That Bob has jinxed me. He's been jinxing me ever since I broke out of jail. I'm going to put some lead into that muchacho one of these mornings."

I said nothing.

When Bob said to me later, "How's your luck? Changed any?" I turned to him and said, "Bob if I was you I'd take off somewhere."

"Why?"

"You know why."

"Suppose you tell me."

"I'm just trying to do you a favor hombre. The Kid thinks you're jinxing him. I wouldn't buck my luck if I was you."

"It's the Kid who's bucking his luck."

"All right. I'm just warning you."

"I know him a hell of a lot better than you do."

"Forget I mentioned it."

"I will," Bob said. He was pretty sore.

We went to some cockfights and to one bad bullfight and then the Kid got restless and we moved down the coast to Ensenada, about sixty miles below. I had never seen such beaches, with great dunes from which you could look far out into the ocean. The Kid at this time was not planning to return to the States—there was hardly a place in the States where he would not be hunted—but he had not made up his mind yet what he would do down in old Mex. We were just resting but I could see that the Kid was beginning to feel like a fish out of water. He had always operated in the States and back there was where he had his real reputation. Mehico was just a little too brand new for him. That was why he got restless in Tijuana, I think. The bad bullfight sort of clinched it. There was this tall American trying to make passes and getting thrown all over the arena and the Kid sneered and I could see it was a bad omen. And the fellow made a mess of the killing and the people shouted and threw bottles. So we went to Ensenada, where we had a few friends, and lay around down there for a while.

Ensenada was only a village and life was very quiet. The Kid got several business propositions in the lines of rustling, smuggling and counterfeiting and so we had no worries about money. Our own money was still holding out. But something was going sour among us and we knew it. The Kid kept to himself a lot and I could see he was mulling over something. And then we started getting sick—Bob first, then the Kid and then Harvey. I didn't get it. They lay around on the little rancho south of Ensenada, throwing up, chasing out to the outhouse, and running a fever and cursing the whole of Mehico for doing it to them. I'll never know to the day I die why I didn't get it too. I've got a pretty tough stomach but it's nothing to the cast-iron one Bob used to have.

Well the Kid got fed up with all this and one morning he said, "Boys I left some unfinished business up north and I'm going up there to finish it."

"What kind?" Harvey asked.

"Dad Longworth business. I've got to go up there and pay him a courtesy call. It's not right my not saying goodbye when I took off. I'm going to tree that town and shoot Dad in the ass. You fellows stay here. It's not your play."

"The hell it isn't," I said. "I got a couple of calls to pay myself."

"That's right," said Harvey.

"What about you Bob?" asked the Kid.

"I don't think we ought to go," said Bob.

"Sure," said the Kid.

"Well you asked me."

"I did."

"There's a price on your head up there. Dad'll be itching to have you come back. He's just hoping you will. Let's stay put for a while."

"Kid it isn't Nika you're going up there for is it?" I asked.

"Maybe," he said.

"Now look Kid I'm with you to the finish," said Bob. "You know that. If you're going up there so am I."

The Kid stared at him a minute, then said, "Sure Bob."

"What makes you think she'll come back with you?" I asked.

"She only married Miguel to gravel me. She'll do what I tell her."

"Jesus and I was just beginning to feel half alive again," I said.

"I haven't asked you to come along."

"I know," I said, "but where would you be without papa?"

He laughed.

"Christ what a ride," I groaned.

And so we started that killing trip all over again.

7

It took us eleven days to make that trip south and twelve to make it back. Counting the fifteen days we spent in old Mex, we were away from the Monterey country thirty-eight days. We left on Friday, June third, and returned on Sunday, July tenth. We spent twenty-three days on horseback and I can tell you I was more saddle-sore on July tenth than I have ever been in my life. I hate to think of how many miles we rode. All I know is that although riding was more natural to us than walking we were not fit to do much hard riding for the next couple of weeks. For myself, I remember that the inside of my thighs and legs were raw, that walking was painful and that my left shoulder blade sometimes woke me at night with its aching.

Going south was one thing. We had been leaving danger behind us with each day. Going north was another. We could be betrayed by some of the people we had to do business with—one of our friends even—who could send a telegram north to tip them off we were coming. By now there was a nice little price of $1,000 on the Kid's head, which made many a trigger finger itchy. But none of us cared about this except

Bob. All the way north he kept hinting to us of the danger of going back but the farther north we went the happier we were. One night Bob said, "Kid it's murder to go up around that Punta."

"Is it?" asked the Kid. "You scared Bob?"

"Kid why do you keep riding me?" Bob asked.

We were all sitting down. The Kid looked Bob over carefully and said, "I'm not riding you Bob," in a voice as soft as velvet. "I love you Bob."

And he laughed in a way which made my back shiver. I thought: Bob you'd best not hang around much longer if you're aiming to stay alive. Bob looked kind of funny and then glanced at me. The Kid walked off into the dark.

"What's eating him?" Bob asked. "What have I done?"

"You know the answer to that one better than we do," Harvey said.

"I've done nothing," said Bob angrily.

"Look Bob," I said, "if I was you I'd just go back to Tijuana and wait until this thing blows over. It's not exactly healthy your riling him."

"I'm not riling him," Bob protested angrily.

"No?" Harvey said.

"Now look Bob," I said.

"No," he said.

"Bob listen," I said.

"No!"

"All right. You're a big boy."

"What do you mean by that?"

"What would I mean? We just got enough trouble the way things are. Haven't we Harvey?"

"Christ," Harvey groaned.

"Well let's forget it," I said.

But of course it was easier said than done.

One evening before supper when I was alone with Harvey I said, "Hey French you notice any change in the Kid?"

"What do you mean?" he said, looking at me.

"He seem the same to you?"

"Sure. Why?"

"I don't know," I said.

"Well if you don't know what are you asking for? What you got on your mind?"

"Nothing. I just wondered."

"Doc where were you when they handed out the brains?"

"I was ahead of you Frenchy."

"Bob been talking to you?"

"No. Why?"

"He's got some crazy notion. I don't know what's got into Bob."

"We're none of us in any too good shape," I said.

"You can say that again Doctor."

Afterward Bob got hold of me and took me aside and said:

"Did I hear you say he wasn't bucking his luck? Well boy when you start playing the game like that there's only one kind of finish and you know what I mean. That calabozo must have done something to him."

"Look Bob," I said, "let me give you a little piece of advice. You're getting to be a pain in the ass."

"You watch your tongue Doc or I'll cut it out for you."

"Not you Robert. You're not big enough. And don't go pushing me because as it is it won't take much for me to cut you in two. I'd be doing the Kid a favor come to think of it."

"All right," Bob said. "You fellows are against me. I don't know what I've done but I see the way the cards are stacked."

"If something happens to the Kid's luck he's going to swear you jinxed it. In that case I wouldn't want to be in your boots."

"All right," said Bob. "I've said all I'm going to say. I wash my hands of the whole thing. I've said my piece and that's it."

"Now you're getting smart," I said.

That same evening, around the supper fire, the Kid suddenly startled us by saying, "I've got it!"

"What?" I asked.

But he went into a burst of laughter, with his head back, his face purple, his lashes very blond, almost invisible, and his strong teeth gleaming. Then he sat there smiling, the muscles playing around his mouth as if they were out of control.

"I'm going to tree that Dad—but good," he said.

"How?" Harvey asked.

"You'll find out."

"Tell us now," I said.

"No."

"You sure?" I asked.

"You going to kill him?" Harvey asked.

"You'll find out," said the Kid.

We laughed about it, even Bob, and kept wondering what the Kid had in mind for old Dad.

Well when we got back to the Monterey country we lay around Old Man Richardson's ranch. He was a big fellow with wiry gray hair and a killer mustache, about forty and a bachelor. He had a small place with a number of Mexican hands. It was a couple of miles south of the Punta and up in the hills a way east of the mission road. He was always friendly to us and we did business with him on a number of occasions. We lay around the first couple of days, even the Kid, just stayed put and slept and ate and slept some more, not caring if it was day or night, and we rubbed ourselves down with whiskey where the skin could take it and with olive oil where the skin was raw. Bob was in bad shape. The thing had got him in the gut again and now he took to his bunk and stayed there. He could not drink anything stronger than water but Harvey and I put away quarts of wine, feeling good only when we were so drunk we could not see straight enough to tell a pumpkin from the moon. The Kid would not touch that stuff but had to throw down that rotgut they called whiskey in that country. The boy was doing his best to ruin himself, that's for sure.

And then, on the morning of Wednesday the thirteenth, he just couldn't keep away from the Punta. To tell the truth I myself wanted to see it again. That tongue of land fascinated all of us, I guess.

When I first got a look at it I wondered why anybody in his right mind would want to live on a place like that and I understood why they had named it Devil's Point—Punta del Diablo, as the natives called it—it being so craggy and wind-beaten and fog-blown, with only one good spring on the whole of it, with crazy wind-shaped trees, and with the bellows of the sealions (seawolves the paisanos called them) heard all over the place when the wind was blowing right. But when I found out that it had small meadows where the grazing was rich and that they did not tilt up on the hills which came pouring down toward them from the east and which ended abruptly just the other side of the mission road, and when I learned that it was a good clean place with good fishing and with several good beaches on the southern side I was ready to believe that my first impression had been wrong.

But even these advantages didn't strike me as being enough to offset the bad points and of course nobody but the very poor would have thought of living there, Indians and greasers and a few Japs and Chinks. I wondered if the poor ever have an ounce of brains in their heads. Some years back a few whalers had used the larger coves for processing whales but that was over with now and only parts of whale skeletons and two gray wooden shacks remained to show they had ever been there. The place didn't make sense for all-around living but even if it didn't there it was, the handful of adobes around the plaza and the occasional adobes out in the meadows and the very rare ones up in the high heads, such as those we lived in, on Hijinio Gonzales' property.

The plaza itself overlooked the largest cove and it was just a flat square piece of land that had been trampled down into hardness by feet and hooves. The dirt was sandy and had crushed shells in it but the loam on top had made it hold and it lay quiet like a cement and hardly ever raised a dust even when a horse stopped suddenly and kicked dirt flying. That was all it was, an old plaza, like so many of the kind you found in the west and south of the border, and it sat on a rise of ground with the adobes thinly spread around it and with walks and trails winding among the houses out to the rest of the sloping meadow. On the northern side of the plaza, closest to the water but with its back to it, was an old adobe larger than the others, with a cross on top and with a yard picket-fenced around it. This was the church, serviced by a padre from the town who came up on a sorrel twice a week. The yard was a burial ground no longer used for that, with old wooden crosses sticking up here and there over the mummy-shaped mounds and occasionally a chunk of stone. When you crossed the plaza going to the church you saw the cove spread out blue behind it.

Nika's adobe was one of those facing the plaza, a middle-sized adobe from the door of which you got a view of the rolling green-yellow meadow backed up by the stand of young pines and behind this the olive Santa Lucia hills. On the left was the church—she married Miguel in it, sick as he was—the inside of which was cool and earth-smelling on the hottest days, with the crisp odors of incense and hot wax. On those hot days the plaza lay shimmering in the bright heat, a flat packed naked square of ground trampled out of the large meadow. Across the plaza, on a slight diagonal from Nika's, was Miguel's place and on the right was the long Vicente adobe, all white, with its long portico facing the plaza.

As for ourselves, we lived as I said on one of the high heads—on the highest one, matter of fact, and the one farthest out into the ocean. It was a spectacular place but you can fool me why anybody would want to build up there. Everything you brought in there had to be carted uphill and the road was not good. I remember asking Hijinio why in hell they had built that place there, with the adobes, barn and so on, but he did not know either. It reminded me of places you read about in Spain, built on hills and mountains as a kind of insurance against anybody jumping you, and come to think of it maybe that's why they built that place like that. There wasn't hardly a spot up there that didn't jut out fifty or a hundred feet over the water and there wasn't a beach anywhere around where you might hide a boat and go out when the going got rough—providing, that is, that you could make it down to the water in the first place, the likely fact being that you'd lose your footing and go smashing down to make food for the gulls and cormorants, or, if you were slow, get yourself a bullet in the back. I had pointed all that out to the Kid on more than one occasion but I might as well have saved my breath for all the good it did. Of course as far as I was concerned the whole damned Punta was a death trap, being a headland, and so I don't know why I bothered to make a fuss about that old cypress head.

There sure were some pretty spots around there—meadows full of paintbrush, coves full of shallow canyons and glassy pools, the thunder of the surf, the starfish lying steaming on the rocks, the big anemones and the big purple urchins, locoweed, sagebrush, buckwheat, lava-gray beaches, bright black and glass-green water—and all the time the smell of fish and seawolves and rotting kelp and fog and bird-droppings, rolling in on the seawinds under the burning light.

The Punta was like a thumb sticking out into the Pacific or like a flattened lizard, the head and legs frayed, with countless coves eaten by the sea. And yet in places it was as sweet and soft as you could dream about. When it was winter in other places it was just a lovely spring there, never any frost or hardly ever, although the nights were cold and the ocean icy. In winter you would find delicate flowers coming up out of a ground that you expected, over and over, to be frozen, and in the summer you almost always got fooled by the ocean when you jumped in.

And the sun was a sun you could really talk about—the same sizzling ball in that inky sky as it was out in the inland ranchos: Los Tularcitos out by Buckeye Ridge, Los Coches and Arroyo Seco south of Soledad, Posa de los Ositos near King City, and all the many other chunks of land that the Spaniards and Mexicans had handed out, not by acres, but by leagues, as though the land were endless. It was the same sun that burned Salt Slough and Tin House Spring and Horsethief Canyon and Quién Sabe Valley and Rattlesnake Creek. The summers I had been used to back around Franklin (now El Paso) and Las Cruces and Deming and Tucson and Phoenix had been so hot you could fry an egg on the top of your head. Nothing but desert there, while out on the Punta and on the ranchos to the north and south it was cool in summer and this was a great surprise to me. It was the sea breeze and the fog that cooled that country off.

As for the fog, it made me feel fenced in and after a couple of days of it I'd get so jumpy I'd want to shoot the first thing that crossed my path, and if you think it was just me let me tell you it affected my sorrel the same way. I have always thought that you could not rightly understand those days unless you understood the effect of the land on a man. Out in the open country of New Mexico you could sit on your horse and ride and ride and camp alone when night came and ride again and sleep alone and ride again. So why should it surprise anybody that that kind of space, which rolls along like the ocean but which seems to have more secrets—down in the gulches and arroyos, in the hills, on the mesas and behind the buttes— could beat a man down until he was fighting mad, so that when he hit a little town he was so edgy it was best you let him be, asked him few questions if any and gave him plenty of room on the street, particularly if you had reason to believe that he liked his gunplay fast and sudden. Hell no wonder a man like that didn't talk much. It was a wonder he knew how to talk at all after whiskey had loosened his jaws a bit. The fog was like that too unless I'm off my target.

Let me tell you a little story they used to tell around there. One night a padre was walking up Devil's Hill, carrying a sack containing a hen and seven chicks. He was bringing the hen and chicks to a poor family in Monterey. When he came to Devil's Elbow it was thick with fog as usual, the clammy heavy fog that you swim around in. Along came a mal hombre and hit him over the head, then took the sack and went into town. But when he got to his house the sack was empty. He went up to the Elbow again and found the hen and chicks picking in the ground near the padre. He put them in the sack and went into town again. Again he found the sack empty. He went up to the Elbow again and saw the hen and chicks still picking in the ground. He felt the padre's heart and saw that he was dead. Then he pointed his gun at his own head and killed himself. And ever since then the Elbow has been haunted and the mission grounds have been haunted too.

I heard an old Indian tell that story. He also told some stories about the mission days. There weren't too many Indians left in that country after what the mission fathers had done. The fathers had saved them and after that the Indians' life was not so good. Once they were baptized they had to live the mission way and if they went back to their old life they were hunted by the soldiers from the presidio and if they were not killed they were brought inside the mission walls and flogged until they had changed their minds. And that's the truth, regardless of what you may have heard.

The death rate among the Indians, after the padres had saved them, was something even the padres worried about, but they did not worry very hard or hard enough, because the mission's wealth and power kept growing, the mission kept getting more and more land, more livestock, more gold, and it did not make much of a difference for the Indians when the Jesuits were pushed out and the Franciscans came in, the death rate did not decrease and the Indians did not have their old life back, the only life that made any sense to them. What they needed was not baptism but guns. By the time the mission fell into ruins there were hardly any more Indians to save, they had slowly disappeared, like the wolves and grizzlies, only the wolves and grizzlies had moved back into the hills, but the Indians had moved back into nothing better than extinction. Maybe the padres hadn't meant to push them out. Maybe they had just done a better job than they had wanted to or counted on. Anyhow that's what I heard the old Indian say.

The Kid took off alone that morning of the thirteenth, went down the mission road, turned off onto the Punta and rode down to the plaza. He went into Nika's adobe but she was not there. Then it occurred to him to go into the church. He led his horse over there, tied it to the fence and walked in. So this was the church she had got herself married in, with the padre, the Latin droning, the incense, the smoke of candles, the crucifixes and madonnas, the paisano paintings frescoed to the walls. They must have paid the padre to ride up from town, the bald fat padre on his sorrel in his cassock.

He went out and rode over to the Big Meadow, then to Little Mound Meadow and over to the South Plateau, but he could not find her. He returned to her adobe and she was still not there. He stood in the doorway, waiting. He had passed several of the paisanos and they had waved to him—quietly, as if he were not a hunted man, as if he were not the Kid himself, as if he had never gone away. They were good people and he was glad to be back.

He watched some men crossing the plaza, going barefooted on their leathery calluses or wearing rough sandals, carrying the great loads on their backs without grunting, one of them toting water in buckets slung on a pole over his shoulders. They scratched in the earth until they died in it and fished in the sea until they drowned in it but they always had time for a baile and for singing in their nasal husky voices and bad as their life was they did not think much about the next day or the next year.

Could he convince her to do what he wanted her to do? She was like a cat and might out-think him all along the way. But what would she want to stay around here for? Without him there was nothing here for a woman with fire and pepper like her and she would only grow old, her face getting more bony, or she would grow fat and the fat would drown the fire in her. He would take her down there and that would be the end of it. Why had he gotten mixed up with her in the first place? What was wrong with the white ones? (What wasn't wrong with them?) They sure must look funny together, he with his sandy head and she with her jet hair, he only a little taller than she and looking a little like a girl himself except for the muscles, and she with her man's face and hard body and brown skin. But he liked the feel and smell of her and could not understand why he had changed her for Juanita, even if it had been a joke, which he wasn't sure about.

He decided he would pay Miguel Gomez a visit. He led his horse across the plaza and tied him to the post in front of Miguel's place. Then he entered the darkness and coolness and saw a man lying on a bunk with the window light falling over his shoulders and at first he thought he had come into the wrong place because the man did not look like Miguel at all and not even like a thinner brother of Miguel. He did not look like anybody at all, only like somebody who had been dug up out of a fresh grave.

"Hi Miguel," he said quietly. "What you want to go and get yourself kicked by a horse for? That's not a smart thing to do."

"Hi Kid," said Miguel weakly, smiling. "I been expecting you."

"Me?" said the Kid.

Miguel had hollow cheeks and hollow eyes and his forehead looked too large and his mustache seemed to have wilted and the face and arms that had been a reddish brown had a yellow tinge and the large eyes were dull and had lots of yellow in the whites. He had been a good-sized fellow, with a plumpish face and good color and sharp eyes and a clean shining mustache, and now look at him.

"How's it been with you Kid?" Miguel asked, in a voice which was hoarse and unlike the voice the Kid remembered.

"Pretty good. You?"

"Not so good."

"So I hear. Too bad."

"That was a great escape," Miguel said.

"It was nothing."

"You couldn't do better. No other man could do better."

"I'm sorry about Patron."

"Yes that's bad. But now everybody says you couldn't help it. They found the gunroom door broke open and figured out what happened."

"How have things been back here?"

"The papers were full of it. They say it was in papers back east too—Missouri, Kansas. They looked for you in the hills and below but found no trace of you. How you like Mehico?"

"How'd you know I was coming?"

"Who said I did?"

"You said you were expecting me."

"Sure but I didn't know the day."

"You knew I was coming back?"

"Sure."

"How come?"

"What would you do down in Mehico Kid? A fellow as light-skinned as you. This is where you make your play."

"How's Nika?"

"Changed. I've changed she's changed you've changed. Lots of changes lately."

"Is that bad?"

"Depends on how you look at it."

"Should you be talking so much?"

"No that's a fact. You been to her place? You been there? Then she's up at Hijinio's, helping to plaster an adobe."

"Thanks."

"Talk to her."

"Sure."

"See what she says."

"Sure."

"What's this business you got with Longworth? You better leave him alone Kid. He's mad as hell—like a bull."

The Kid shrugged.

"Hombre you watch yourself. You've changed too," Miguel said.

"I know. I'm getting fed up with the whole thing."

"Still drinking that rotgut?"

The Kid nodded.

"That's bad."

"Everything's bad. Your getting kicked by a horse is bad."

"You're driving yourself hard. Where you going?"

"You tell me," the Kid said, smiling.

"Funny way for you to talk."

"I talk the way it comes."

"How's it down there?"

"The old country?"

"Yes."

The Kid shrugged. "How should it be? Same everywhere—people living, dying."

"Long trip?"

"Too long."

"Maybe too long for the business you've come for."

"No. I've come on the business of my life."

"Big words. I never heard you talk like that."

"A fellow changes."

"Up or down?"

The Kid smiled. "It happens in the dark."

"Some can see in the dark."

"I'm one of the daytime boys."

Miguel laughed softly, watching the Kid.

"How'd you know I was back?" asked the Kid. "You knew didn't you?"

"News travels fast. What do you expect?"

"Nothing."

"That's good. It's the best way to live."

"And to die."

"You know I'm dying then?"

"You? Nobody told me."

"Why should they?"

"Are you really dying?"

"Why? Is death so surprising to you?"

"Sometimes," said the Kid.

"That's funny."

"What happened to you?"

"A dumb story. One of my cousin's mares kicked me in the chest. A week later I began spitting blood. I guess it was the kick that did it."

"How'd you let a mare kick you?"

"I don't know. I was working in the stable and was going to pass her. She reared up ... and hit me in the chest. It threw me down. I thought she was going to come for me but she shied. Went to a corner. I guess it frightened her."

"It can happen."

"I never got kicked like that before. Not like that. In the shins, in the thigh, but nothing serious. It wasn't a bad kick just kind of grazed me. Didn't break anything but I didn't feel good. Then I began spitting blood."

"Ever spit blood before?"

"When I was a kid. Also when I was about eighteen."

"Maybe the kick had nothing to do with it."

"I don't know."

Miguel sighed and looked at his hands, which were lying still and bony on the blanket. Then he glanced up at the Kid. The Kid had been standing at the foot of the bed, his hands in his back pockets.

"I been waiting for you Kid," he said. "I knew you'd come. I knew it all the time, ever since I saw I wasn't going to die right away."

"You think I came back just for Nika?"

"I don't know. I wonder if you'd have come back if I had died or if I hadn't gone and married her."

"I'd have come back."

"Kid the padre made her mine. The padre's word is God's. I took her in the sight of God."

"Sure. I haven't said a word."

"But I didn't expect to live. Only I wanted to marry her and leave her the little I've got. It's not my fault I didn't die. But you know something? She won't go back with you now, not while I'm alive. Listen. Go back. You'll get your death here. She's wild. Like you. You need a tame one. She'll get you killed. She can do that to a man. But me I'm her cousin. And I'm dying anyway."

"What makes you so sure?"

"I can feel it. Listen. I'm sorry now I did it. I'm no husband to her. There were two things I counted on—you dying and me dying—and we're both alive. Ah Christ. I loved her a long time without telling her. There was always some fellow or other but she didn't seem to want to marry them and I guess now it was because of one thing but it's not for me to say what. A woman will seem to do strange things if you don't know what's in her mind. You understand?"

The Kid nodded.

"She says she loves me. I believe her. Love can come from suffering just as easy as from fun. We're cousins. That counts with us. You know—she's always feeling blue because she doesn't have much kin. Her brother Modesto's the only one who's really close to her except me and I'm a second cousin. Her mother had three children. One died young. Nika was the second. They lived in that adobe on the plaza and a couple of years ago her father got drowned—he was a fisherman—and her mother (God bless her, she was a good woman and she always worried about me) died a couple of months after—a stroke. That left Nika alone with her brother. She was always talking about leaving the Punta but she never did. I sure didn't want to see her go."

He paused. "You see what I mean?"

"Sure," said the Kid.

"But it makes no difference."

"That's right," said the Kid.

"Well she had a house and she worked here and there and

I thought of asking her to marry me but she was a wild one and had other fellows and anyway after my wife died I didn't want to marry anybody for a long time. I don't know why I'm telling you all this. I guess when a man has nothing better to do than to spit blood and try to hang on to his life he talks more than is good for him. It's good to see you. I'm glad they didn't hang you."

"Me too." The Kid laughed.

"You better go up and talk to her."

"Sure. Well so long."

"Adiós Kid. Look out for the Dedricks."

"I will. Take care of yourself. Adiós."

As he mounted his horse and rode up toward Hijinio's he could not help remembering how Miguel had looked in the old days. Such a nice fellow then, brown-skinned, sharp black eyes, lots of curly black hair, and a very good build on him, not too much fat for a fellow his age. But a funny fellow Miguel. He had never worn a gun in his life. Never owned a gun. Said he never needed one. That was taking a lot on trust wasn't it? Too bad he was dying.

After the Kid took off that morning I went over to Harvey and said, "Harvey you know what? You and me ought to follow him a bit just in case there's any trouble and anyway we ought to scout around a bit."

"Good idea," said Harvey, and we got on our horses and rode off north. The surprising thing was that it felt good to be on a horse again.

We rode on past the Punta and then, not knowing exactly what we were there for or what to do, I said, "Let's go over to the Pescadero and Punta Pinos."

"What for?"

"I don't know."

"All right let's go," he said.

He was about twenty-two and tall and thin and had a narrow face and gray eyes that were very shiny and a brown cowlick and a clump of hair that hung down over his eyes and he was a very good cowhand but not so good at staying alive. Because the day we took that ride was the day he got himself killed. One thing about Harvey I can never forget—the way he had of laughing. He would lie down on his stomach and writhe and make hacking noises as if somebody was cutting him up with a knife. What will make a fellow develop a habit like that?

"Harvey," I said as we rode along, "what do you aim to do when this blows over?"

He scratched his head. "You got me Doc," he said. "What do you say we hit the beach?"

"All right."

We turned off near the mission and rode onto the beach. The horses didn't like that. They began to rear and buck and we hit them with our reins and made them quit it. There was nobody on the beach, only the muddy flat where the river joined the bay. We splashed through it, the water going into our boots. We climbed the hill there, with the view of the bay, the mission ruins and the Punta, and the horses breathed hard, their sides heaving, and they farted and stopped a minute and we waited for them.

It was good country in those days, full of eagles and hawks. You never got tired of riding around in it. One minute you'd be riding through those mossy trees and the next you'd be skirting a head and watching a line of cormorants sitting black on a rock or you'd see the black water in the rock scars and wonder how deep it was down there and if anybody had been thrown in there. Or you'd pass the long snaking brown lines out near the kelp beds and hear the blowing water and watch the crazy cypresses that the poet said look like a witch's fingers, pale gray, with blue shadows.

We went north and headed all the way up toward the Restless Sea and there you could see the change in the land— no more great rocks except offshore and plenty of sandhills and scrub pine and browning grass and yellow trails and grazing cattle and you could taste the saltmist on your tongue. It was up in those sandhills that the Kid later killed and buried Bob Emory. Nowadays they use that sand to make cement, I am told, and have a big factory there.

We rode down onto the beach again and saw the seawolves poking their heads like bald old Negroes out of the water. The rotting kelp on the beach stank of iodine and terns flew up in clouds and cried in their high voices and we rode through the millions of flies and tasted the bitterness in our mouths and watched the ocean boiling around the rocks and the sunlight prickling off it. Well if you were going to get yourself killed it was as good a spot as any in that country. Come to think of it, that was the last time I ever went out to that point near Spanish Bay. I wouldn't want to go back, though. I understand they've got it all changed, the way they always have.

The Kid found Nika up around Hijinio's and got off his horse when he saw her. There were two other women with her, working the outside of the adobe, but the others left when they saw him coming, and Nika just stood there, her hands full of mud, and watched him come, the anger showing in her face. He came up close, leading his horse, and stopped and stared at her.

He sensed that she had changed. She looked different—tired, a little grim, and almost as if she had been drunk for a long time. She looked older too. He knew that he would have his troubles with her. In a way she was no longer the Nika he had known and yet her face and figure had hardly changed at all. Watching her, he was glad he had come to get her. She was as peppery as ever. She stood with her hands on her hips, her head held arrogantly and her jet hair showing a little on her forehead from under the small rebozo which fell and covered her shoulders. Her face was gaunt. He liked that too. The cheeks were high, Indian-like, the eyes deepset beneath bony brows, the nose strong and the nostrils flaring, the mouth large, with a downward sweep of arrogance, and her cheeks were sunken, the whole face a little skull-like.

There was something about her all right. She was not as pretty as some of the other girls but she had fire. He did not like the soft round ones with the slightly flabby faces or the faces just beginning to turn flabby, with the flattish Indian faces and the Mongolian eyes, or the soft young ones with faces like plums. He knew them and he knew that past a certain point there was no fun in them, although they had their own kind of pepper too. He was getting too old for the soft ones. He liked this woman standing there as though she were ready to turn her back on him or to spit in his face or to cut him up with a knife. She had beautiful hands, long and almost wristless, the lean forearms flowing darkly onto them and the fingers clean and long and straight. They were the hands of a murderer and he liked them.

Why had he gone after other women? Why had he hurt her? He felt a little dizzy. Was it because he was tired or was it because of her effect on him? A woman like this could last a man a long time. And yet he had hurt her, had brought the girl Juanita here and had let her live with him for more than a week, the soft Juanita from the hills, with the moon face, the almost light skin, the black hair and black eyes, the soft nubby nose and the dimpled cheeks, the soft shoulders and the child-like glances, the soft mouth with the curling corners and the crying spells when she thought he was displeased with her.

"You had no right to do it while I was still alive," he said.

"What are you doing back?" she asked.

"You got married on Wednesday but I was not supposed to be dead until Saturday. You thought I was gone for sure. You wrote me off for dead both of you."

"Oh cut it out!" she cried. "If that's what you've come to tell me save your breath!"

"On Wednesday I was still alive. If I had made a break and got myself killed for my trouble it would have been all right for you to get yourself married. But on Wednesday I was still alive."

"Yes? And what about that Juanita?"

"You were still my woman, regardless. And you should have come and told me. You should have come anyway, even if you didn't tell me, knowing I was waiting for my death."

"Now wait a minute. I was going to come."

"But you thought I was as good as dead and not worth bothering about. It's wrong to write a man off before his time—you know that? That must have been some wedding night, him sick in his lungs and you sick in your heart."

"You keep him out of it!"

"Why? Because he stole my woman?"

"You keep him out of it!"

"I wouldn't want to remember that wedding night if I was you. The padre that married you ought to be ashamed of himself and if I'm ashamed of some of the things I've done, like bringing that girl here and shaming you, I'm not as ashamed as that padre ought to be and you too. But let's forget all that and start from scratch in old Mex. This country is not good for us any more. What do you say? Will you come back with me?"

"You go to hell," she said.

"I want you down there with me. The country is good. Miguel won't try to hold you. He knows you belong to me. He married you behind my back but I don't hold it against him. When a man wants a woman anything goes. He's a nice fellow but he's dying. You know that?"

"Stop talking like that!" she cried, furious with him. Then she said softly, "Why didn't you die? Why did you come back to haunt us? I have no use for you. Understand?"

"Sure you have," he said. "I know you."

"Do you? I got a brother and a husband and a house. A house my father built. I was born here. I like this country. Where were you born Kid?"

He smiled.

"You don't know?" she said.

"No."

"Who was your mother?"

He shrugged.

"You don't know that either? I remember my mother and my father and this is where they lived and where I've lived and I'm sick of strangers."

"You calling me a stranger?"

"That's right! You go from place to place, killing, always afraid of being killed. What do you think it would be like living with you? Sure. You kill Patron, Dedrick. But they're bound to get you. And what about the others? The other killers? Always waiting to catch you drunk or with a hangover or a little sick in the stomach or with your eyes bloodshot or with your shooting arm stiff? You think they're dead? There's always a new one coming up and getting ready to put that one bullet into you. Where would I be in all that?"

"You've done all right," he said.

"Have I? I'm tired of all that. Miguel's sick. I've got all I can do to keep him alive. He needs me and I need him and the truth is you never need anybody."

"All right," he said dryly, smiling.

She was not the only one who had changed. He had changed too and she saw it. His face was raw from the sun and wind, his eyes bloodshot, and he was tired down into his bones and it showed in the way he walked—there was a kind of brittleness in his gestures—and in the slow tired way his bright lashes settled down over his eyes and in the way the corner of his mouth turned down slightly as if in irritation. He had always been a clean fellow, he had always bathed whenever he could and had liked to use lots of soap, but now the grime had settled into the hairline creases of his neck and in some apparently new lines of his face, which suddenly showed the years on him, and she noticed these things and was surprised. She saw that he was not so much of a boy any longer and she knew he would not live to reach his next birthday. As long as he had been a boy no one could kill him but now he was done for, she thought.

"You'd better get out of this country if you want to stay alive," she said. "And if you do anything to Miguel God help you."

"All right," he said. "I've had it coming. Miguel give you that ring?"

"You sure didn't," she said bitterly. "You just took off."

"How about forgiving a fellow?" he asked.

"What are you smiling about?" she said.

"Well?" he asked softly.

She refused to answer.

"Looks like I'm not exactly popular around here," he said.

"And why should you be?" she demanded. "Just who do you think you are?"

He shrugged.

"Me? Nobody," he said and turned and walked away toward his horse, going in that new brittle way which told her that he was very tired and beginning to feel his age and hadn't long to live.

I never did like that Nika much. I didn't like the way she wore her hair and the way she talked up in her nose. She wore her hair long and parted exactly in the middle, with the ends braided and coiled tight at the back of her head, and she wore it with her head up and with that tight skin of her face which showed the bones underneath and with her strong nose which always looked as if she were flaring her nostrils and with her large teeth bulging against her closed lips (making you think she was using snuff), and when she walked around like that I hated her. After all she was no better than a slut and had no right to put on airs.

As I said, when she talked it was always up in her nose. Everybody else talked in their mouth or back in their throat but this wasn't good enough for Nika, she had to get that whine into it. And when she said something to you in that high whiny voice you would have thought, if you had been the damn fool she took you for, you heard an angel talking, the way she turned those large black eyes on you and the way she dropped her lids or twisted her lips into a smile or puckered the papery skin on the front of her cheeks or showed you her long white teeth and the tip of her hot tongue or placed her bony hand on the crown of her head.

The Kid had taught her to shoot pretty well and she even liked to fool around with snap shooting and drawing from the hip, but that was because they were in "love." She was the kind of woman who took up whatever her man was good at or that she thought he was good at or that somebody had convinced her he was good at. As for their being in love, it was a funny kind of love that could make people act like that toward each other, especially that could make a woman ruin a good man. Her walk was good and her body was good too—she was thin and wiry and small-breasted and could punch you with bony fists and make you feel it—and she had some kind of style but she also had something murderous, you never knew which way she was going in love or in hate, and I'm positive she didn't know either and maybe that's why the Kid took to her the way he did.

She was a fourflusher from way back and I'll give you ten to one that if she's still alive she's fourflushing right now. She was the kind of woman who could get hold of a peaceful man and in no time flat make a murderer out of him. She would have done that to Miguel if she had had the time. I have known men who might as well go at their wives with a knife and get it over with but who just pare a little off at a time or who stick the point in here and there to see if the wives can still feel it, which they always can. These men make wrecks of their wives and then blame them for being the wrecks that they made them. Even Miguel would have gotten to be like that, Miguel with the soft skin and the dark gentle eyes and the soft easygoing voice.

He was a nice fellow and in a way he was lucky he died shortly afterward. When he was well he would go over to his piece of land on Headland Meadow and work it and make corn grow there and potatoes and cabbages and beets. He had a cow too and several pigs and a couple of horses that were no better than plugs. I remember him bending over his earth, the sea behind him, his hips heavy, his face a little round, with the black mustache above the heavy lips, and I remember his soft brown hands with the heavy, horny, dirty nails, the earth still on them after he was through working for the day.

One day, after a raid on the Rancho San José y Sur Chiquito, I brought him two good horses and told him he could have them. He did not want to take them.

"Go on take them," I said. "We've changed the brands."

After thinking a long while he said, "All right," and I was glad.

We met the Kid as he was coming off the Punta. I asked him if he wanted to go abalone fishing with us and he said sure, so we went down to a cove we knew on the Punta, where there were lots of abalones hanging on to the rocks, letting the tide drift over them and getting their food from what it brought. The best way to get them was to use a heavy knife, get the point in quick and pry. If you used wood they crushed it. With a knife you could force them loose and lay them with the wet meat and muscle looking skyward. The big ones weighed several pounds. It was good eating after it was pounded, delicate and not very fishy.

We had some fun diving for them and then we rested. The bay was very blue and I could feel the sweat running down my back. On the other side of the bay was the mission church, with its short yellow walls and long red roof. Even at that distance you could see it was a ruin.

"They say the Jesuits built that place," Harvey said.

"You mean the Franciscans," said the Kid.

"No the Jesuits."

"Franciscans."

"I don't know anything about it," Harvey said.

"You and me both," the Kid said, slapping him on the back, and they laughed.

The fog rolled in and then the bay was dead-gray and glassy, the subdued sea spreading out from the cove, the kelp, brown and knobby, heaving offshore, the olive hills showing through the wisps. There were no seasmells then, no smells of anything, and the air was dead except for a faint gull cry and the echoes the seawolves set up, coughing, barking, grunting.

"Be good to get back to Mexico," Harvey said.

"Be good to get back to a drink," the Kid said. "Let's go over to Hijinio's."

We took the outer trail with the sheer drops and found Hijinio and had some aguardiente and the fog lifted and we sat under the cypresses, talking and watching the seawolves on the rocks.

"Good country," said the Kid.

"You been here a long time?" I asked Hijinio.

"Since I was born," he said.

"Where you ever been to in your life?" I asked.

"I been to Paso Robles."

"You ought to go to Mehico. Great country," I said.

It was a pretty spot all right, with those crazy trees gnarled and ashy and none much bigger than an orange tree. They had soft gray trunks and their arms looked wild and frozen. The water slopped below us and every once in a while we would get the stink of fish and droppings.

I have sometimes wondered what you would find if you dug down in his grave. A few yellow bones, I reckon. I remember the way they carried him to the ghost tree, all dressed out after the wake, with Francesca Zamora crying and Hijinio walking behind her, and I remember the sound of the spade as Jesús Garcia dug the grave. He was sweating. When he stopped for a rest somebody said, "Deeper Jesús deeper. It isn't right to leave a man so shallow."

"Don't you think I know how to bury a man?" said Jesús Garcia angrily.

And I remember that Nika was not there—she was lying shocked on the Kid's bed—and Miguel was dying and Harvey was dead and Bob was dead and now the Kid was dead and there was only me left, and I had the feeling that I had better take off and start life from scratch somewhere else, and it was a hot night in the middle of July, with no trace of fog and with a full moon that lighted our way, and the seawolves were barking and I remember how we left the place, after Jesús Garcia had filled the grave, each one going quietly, alone.

It must be the same place still. I doubt if you'll find more than half a dozen changes that the years have brought.

8

We rode back to Old Man Richardson's, had some chow and took our siesta. After siesta we went hunting in the hills and Harvey shot a buck, which we brought down to the ranch. Modesto Machado, Nika's brother, was there, waiting to see the Kid.

"Muchacho!" said the Kid, delighted, walking up to Modesto and clapping him on the back.

"Kid! Great to see you!" said Modesto.

They went off to one side, talking, and later the Kid told me Modesto had brought word Dad had heard a rumor he the Kid was back in the Monterey country. It didn't bother the Kid at all. I saw them go out to one of the corrals and target shoot. Modesto showed the Kid how fast he could draw. They talked about some fine points of gunplay, Modesto's eyes glowing as he watched the Kid.

He was sixteen, a nice-looking boy in a Mexican sort of way. He had a small head and clean-looking ears and a lean jaw and a strong chin and a very full mouth and high cheekbones and was very dark and had a wild-growing mustache and his hair was black and soft and grew down over his ears and down his neck and he could look sadder, when the mood hit him, than any other kid I can remember, bending his head so the bottom of his chin was lost in the folds of his serape and looking at you with those soft black eyes under the heavy eyebrows, his mouth slightly open and the upper part of his chin kind of puckered. If there was anybody the Kid really cared about I guess it was this Modesto Machado. Modesto lived in the valley with a Mexican farmer for whom he worked and was a popular boy over there. Sometimes the Kid and I would go to see him and we would stay at the rancheria screened by cottonwoods in the foothills. The Kid had given Modesto his first gun, a nickel-plated Colt's forty-five, and had taught him to shoot, to draw and to take care of the weapon.

They came back from the corral and joined me and Harvey. Modesto said the Dedrick boys had sworn to get the Kid and had shot their mouths off about what they would do to him when they caught up with him.

"Fourflushers," the Kid said. "Fellows that talk before they make their play. Hey Doc you see this kid draw?"

"Sure," I said.

"Practice," said the Kid. "Like this." And he showed him, over and over again. "Now you do it," he said. We watched Modesto.

I once saw Modesto with his right hand bleeding from practice. The Kid would not even let him wipe it. Another time I saw him with his shoulder aching so hard he could barely lift his arm, but the Kid said, "Up there up there. Let's develop those muscles," and Modesto winced and did what he was told.

They say that great gunmen are born great. All I know is that I practiced almost every day and that the Kid practiced and that Wyatt Earp and Doc Holliday practiced.

"Go ahead. Some more," said the Kid.

Modesto had the posture of a matador, with the bent shoulders and flat chest and the curve in the back of the neck, and when he practiced drawing he reminded me of one.

Modesto began to laugh.

"What are you laughing about?" asked the Kid, smiling.

"Remember how you made me wear this forty-five for fourteen hours?"

The Kid smiled.

Modesto turned to me. "He made me wear it everywhere I went. When I took it off my right leg sort of kicked around. Without your gun you feel empty. Savvy?"

I laughed. "Savvy muchacho."

"I don't like the Dedrick boys talking like that," Modesto said.

"To hell with the Dedricks," said Harvey. "How about knocking them off Kid?"

"That's not a bad idea," said the Kid.

"Hunting's good I see," said Modesto, studying the buck.

"Stay for dinner," said the Kid.

"Sorry but I got to be back."

"Listen," said the Kid. "One time a fellow came looking for me, saying what he was going to do to me. He was in a tendejón, bragging, and sent a man to find me and tell me what I was going to get. So I went over to this tendejón to see the fellow. But I didn't hurry. The more this fellow talked the more of his fight he was using up. He was a good fighter out of Abilene and I had to be careful. I checked my gun and loosened it in the holster. 'You the Kid?' he asked me. 'That's what they call me.' 'I'm going to kill you.' 'Well make your play and get it over with,' I said. And I started walking toward him, watching his right hand, waiting for it to telegraph something to me. But it froze. He couldn't get himself to draw. I grabbed him by the seat of his pants and threw him into the street and told him if I saw him in that town again I'd kill him. He went."

"Why didn't you kill him?" asked Modesto.

The Kid shrugged. "Sometimes it's better not to. By making a monkey out of him I hoped to discourage somebody else who might be thinking of killing me for a reputation."

"But he might have shot you next time he got a chance."

The Kid shrugged again. "That would have been *his* good luck."

By the time Modesto left it was late afternoon and we roasted and ate some of the buck and napped for a while. Then the Kid said he was going to the Punta and I knew it was to see Nika again. Harvey and I said we would go along because we wanted to check our stores and arms. We rode onto the Punta and separated, the Kid going down to the plaza and Harvey and I going up to the cypress head. We went over to Hijinio's and told him what we were there for then went to the barn behind his adobe. We had enough stuff there to hold off a small army and as you know that head was full of caves, almost impassable trails, mesquite and sheer drops, where it would be hard to smoke out a man with a gun.

We went back and chewed the fat with Hijinio. He had the biggest adobe up there, overlooking the cove. The one farthest out was the Kid's. I stopped in to check the Kid's and it looked the same—just an empty adobe with a bunk and a few odds and ends and a madonna. My own adobe was just to the right and somewhat behind the Kid's. Harvey and Bob shared one behind the barn. Hijinio had a nice place up there—corrals, a stable and some meadows.

We rode beyond Mound Meadow and climbed down to one of the beaches. There was a kind of pebbly sand there and the water was calm and there were sea caves and sandstone buttes and mesas and castles and no mosquitoes and sometimes the fireflies came and the children ran and laughed. We talked about what we would do in a couple of years. Harvey said he would probably quit this territory and go someplace and get himself a ranch. I said I had similar ideas, only I also wanted to go prospecting.

"Only thing is," I said, "I got a hunch I'm not going to stay alive long enough."

"Jesus I haven't had me a woman in years," Harvey said.

"What about that tamale in Tijuana? What you call that?"

"She bites. Wonder what Nika's doing for a man now."

"Why don't you ask her?"

"She good in bed?"

"How would I know?"

"Who you kidding? I know more than you think I do."

I stared at him. "You must have been eating some of that locoweed."

He laughed. "You think I was born yesterday? You were sleeping with her when he was in that Salinas jail."

I smiled. "Guessing games," I said. But he was right.

"How about going up and talking with Francesca? Get the news."

"All right," I said.

We found her in her son-in-law's adobe on the plaza, where she lived.

"Hello boys," she said.

"Hi Grandma," Harvey said.

"What you know that's good?" she asked.

"Nothing much," I said. "Have you seen the Kid?"

"How should I? He's too busy with that whore."

"Is that a way to talk?" asked Harvey.

"What would *you* call her?" she asked me.

"Me?"

"She's a whore. You know it."

"I don't know," I said.

"Well you do Harvey. Is she a whore?"

"Don't put the finger on *me* Grandma. I don't know a thing about it," he said.

"Somebody should have slit her throat long ago."

"What you got against her Grandma? I thought you forgave her for marrying Miguel," Harvey said.

"She's no good that's all."

"So I gather," I said.

"What do I care about her? How you like Mehico you fellows?"

"Only one trouble down there," said Harvey.

"What?"

"Too many Mexicans."

"Crazy. You're crazy to come back so soon and let him hang around here. What you trying to do, get him killed?"

"He's no baby."

"What you standing out here for? Don't you want to come in?"

"What's the matter with outside?" said Harvey.

"They're over on that hill right now. I heard them arguing. That's what happens. It goes to your head and then you start making mistakes and first thing you know they're throwing dirt in after you."

"What are you so gloomy about?" I said.

"I'm just telling you. There have been fellows up from town, snooping around. Spies."

"Can you prove they're spies?" asked Harvey.

"What kind of question is that? We ought to shoot them. That's what we'll do."

"Good," said Harvey.

"No it's bad. The Kid ought to lay out. They never do. They keep coming back until they get killed."

"All right. We all will," I said.

"I don't give a damn about you," she said. "The Kid's different. I don't want him to get killed."

"Well maybe none of us will," said Harvey.

"That I'd like to see," she said and started laughing.

Francesca was old enough to be the Kid's grandmother, which was something you could tell by just looking at her. None of the natives knew her age and nor did Francesca but she was plenty old. I suppose she was seventy at the time she laid the Kid out for his wake and that would have made her a child when the mission was still pretty new. Anyhow she had a square flat face, a very dark face, with little bunches of loose fat and thousands of fine wrinkles and although it was not a pretty face it was a good one and by that I mean you could look at it for a long time without its turning sour on you. Although it was a square face it had no sharp lines to it, everything being round, like the roundness of her forehead merging into her eyes, and the roundness of her nose against the roundness of her cheekbones, and the roundness of her chin against the roundness of her jaws. She was an Indian woman and some of them have faces like that.

I can remember her clearly, almost always sitting (she used to say, "How long you expect one pair of legs to carry an old no-good woman?"), and with a calico dress of no color or pattern that went down to her ankles and that hung around her like an old sheet and that could have stood some washing, and with the old wrecks of shoes, and with no stockings, and with the old brown fine-wrinkled dirty hands with the long nails that were black, and with the hidden eyes in the round brows and round cheekbones and with the deep soft voice that surprisingly enough did not show much age.

You can search me why the Kid and she ever took to each other but they did. He would always call her Grandma and she would call him Kid and My Kid and Chivato and you could see them sitting in front of her daughter's adobe and talking together, the children running around them dirty and half naked. Sometimes, after a long ride, the first thing he did on hitting the Punta was to look her up. He would ride up to her adobe, his horse sweating and he himself dusty and wearing the black woolen trousers and the scuffed boots and the black woolen shirt and the black sombrero with the trimmings mostly gone from wear, and he would let out a whoop and she'd come out into the light, squinting and grinning, waddling out in that way of hers, like an old goose, and she would shout, "Hey Chivato!"

And he'd say, "What's new Grandma?"

"I'll tell you what's new boy," she'd say. "My Chivato is back. Hop down and eat something."

And he would tie up his horse and go in and have some tortillas or enchiladas or some frijoles which she would make for him. And they'd have coffee together and talk, him stinking from the long ride. This habit of seeing Francesca first used to irritate Nika and she would say, "What do you see in that old Indian bitch?" He would laugh and light a cigarette and say nothing. She would say, "Well you can answer can't you?" but he would only laugh. And if she pushed him beyond that he would turn his back on her and, still laughing, walk away, his guns hanging loose and his spurs clanking softly and his small hips swaying almost like a woman's.

After visiting Francesca he would go to his own place and clean up, get dressed in the soft-collared white shirt and the black string tie and the black cutaway jacket and black woolen trousers and the fancy soft-skinned boots. With his hair wetted down, and rolling a cigarette, he would stroll about the place, ready to listen, saying little, and always wearing the guns and never standing or sitting where his back would make a good target. During the times we lived in the hills he liked to come down to the Punta like that. And in the old days he liked to come into Monterey like that and to sit in the plazas or have a coffee in a small dark shop or to listen to someone talking in an enclosed garden. He liked the braided trousers and the cloaks of the men and the little newspaper and the servants and the adobes that were long and complicated and that had two floors and the New England porticos in front.

I remember once how he bought Francesca a new dress.

"You think I'm going to fool myself up with that?" she said.

"Take it."

"What for? So you dress me in it when I'm dead?"

"Why not?"

"I don't die that soon."

"Well give it to somebody."

She took it but never wore it.

He also bought her several long strings of silver beads, with crucifixes, and these she wore all the time.

There was one thing about her I didn't like and that was the lies she was always telling. She claimed, for example, that the

Kid's first load of buckshot had not killed Dedrick and that the Kid had said, "Well Lon how'd you like another?" And she claimed that the Kid had killed a man for every year of his life. Lots of people took a lie like that for the gospel truth. He had killed only sixteen men at the time and even that figure was uncertain, for some of the men he had left for dead might have recovered. She said he kept notches on his gun. Another lie. Any real gunfighter knew that a notchkeeper was another word for a fourflusher. She said he had a beautiful singing voice which spellbound all the senoritas. The only thing she left out was the guitar. He had a nice voice but nothing special. And what did he need a beautiful voice for when it was his hands that were remarkable, the way they flashed up out of nowhere and never seemed to aim and yet always hit a mortal mark. In the end she had her way and many of the lies stuck. Now when I hear the stories about him I can't believe that anybody in his sound mind would be willing to believe they could all be about just one human being.

Look, I knew him better than most. I fought side by side with him, killed with him, watched some of our boys die with him, lived with him on the grub we had in the hills. Francesca said he was a great man because he shared his wealth with the poor. I'm not aiming to cut the Kid down but just what wealth was she talking about? If he gave a native a cow did that mean he was sharing his wealth? There was plenty more where that had come from and he hadn't worked very hard to get it. The truth is the truth and we might just as well keep it fixed in the record.

*

The Kid found Nika squatting like an Indian woman out-side her adobe, making tortillas in the little round clay oven. Christ, what the hell do I want with her? he thought.

"I saw Modesto just a little while ago," he greeted her as he rode up.

"Hi Hendry," she said.

He dismounted and held the reins loosely.

"He's in good shape," he said. "How come you're making these things so late?"

"It's not so late."

"Can I talk to you?"

"Sure. Look I'm sorry about the way I spoke to you." She glanced up at him. She was still squatting and using her hands.

"That's all right."

"I didn't expect you back so soon."

"I didn't have much to do at Richardson's. Not much for me and the boys to do at the moment."

"How you fixed for money?" she asked.

"Need some? I can get you some."

"You think I'd take money from you?"

"Now don't get sore."

"No. Don't get sore," she said.

"We're all right. Just resting up. Not in business at the moment, you might say."

"What you do down in Mex?"

"Nothing much."

"I'll bet," she said.

"Sure. I was a good boy."

"Sure."

"Well what do you say?"

She stood up and looked at him seriously.

"Look Hendry," she said. "You think I can just leave him? Even if he said I could, if he said, Forget we were married, we had no right to do it while the Kid was still alive. Even then I couldn't."

"Why?"

"Because I love him. You just wanted to use me. To have fun with. But Miguel doesn't think of me like that."

"He must be sick bad," said the Kid.

"He sure is."

"What exactly's the matter with him?"

"God only knows," she said.

"You have the doctor up from town?"

"Sure."

"What'd he say?"

"Gave him some powders."

"Those doctors," the Kid said. "How'd he let a horse kick him like that?"

"I don't know. You know he works for his cousin up in the hills. Probably working too hard. That damned Christiano. It was a Friday, the thirteenth. A black day. Miguel was not feeling so good. That's when one of the mares kicked him. And then on the nineteenth, the following Thursday, he began spitting blood. The spitting was bad but after a couple of days it stopped. Then, on Tuesday, the day I was supposed to come see you, he woke up with a fire in his lungs and we thought he was dying. He asked me to stay with him. I couldn't refuse. Then he asked me to marry him. You were going to die anyway and it didn't seem like much for me to do for him. He's my cousin. I would have done it only for that and because he was dying, but I respect him and now I know I love him. His first wife died while having a baby. Baby died too. It broke Miguel up that thing. And me—you know I can't have kids. What? You didn't know? It's always been like that with me. Well that's the story. Except I swear I was going to come to see you on Friday, the day you escaped."

"I'm sorry about Miguel—about everything," he said. "Look how about taking a walk?"

She glanced ruefully at the oven, wiped her hands on a rag and went with him toward the hill west of the plaza, he leading his horse. When they reached the top of the hill they could see the coves and the bay. They stood there awhile saying nothing.

"Well that's that," he said.

"I'm sorry Hendry," she said.

"But I didn't come back to haunt you like you said. Miguel's no husband to you. Hell I'll marry you too if that's what you want. And I'll be a man to you and won't lie around dying and spitting blood when it's a man you want to make love to you at night."

"You stop that!"

"What you got that body for?"

"You know nothing but your own pleasure."

"It's good enough for me."

"Listen it's time you heard a few things," she said angrily. "You said I counted on your being hung. Well it's not my fault they caught you and not my fault you got away. Listen. I'm no good for you. I never was. We were made to hurt each other. With Miguel it's different. You know what all the paisanos were saying? That I was dragging you down the street of bitterness. That I was making you old before your time, ruining you with too much loving and bad whiskey. That I was going to get you killed. It's true."

"I pay no attention to what other people think."

She turned away.

"Nika," he said softly.

She turned to face him and began to cry, covering her face with her long hands. She had not expected him to speak so softly and to look so much older and so tired. Her thoughts were in a whirl. So much had happened... and now she was Miguel's wife... and she had loved the Kid... and he had made a great escape... and now was back again... and looking so old... and she knew that if she didn't go south with him he would stay and get himself killed...

He watched her, careful not to touch her, careful not to say a word while she wept. She sniffled, wiped her face with her rebozo and turned and went away. He thought he heard her sobbing. He slowly followed her, sighing. What did he want to get mixed up with a brown girl for? Weren't there enough white ones around? He shrugged and forced the thought out of his mind.

*

He joined us down at Francesca's.

"Kid what's this I hear about you?" she asked.

"I don't know Grandma what do you hear?" he said, dismounting.

"You know what."

"Do I?"

"Sure."

"Suppose you tell me," he said, facing her.

"This business of sending word to Longworth you're back."

"What about it?"

"You crazy? Chivato what's got into you? You don't have enough to do. Why don't you find yourself a nice girl? What you want to bother Longworth for?"

"Oh so you're in love with him," he said, grinning.

"Didn't you know? He's going to marry me."

"I'd like to see the kids you two would make."

"Is it true?" she asked.

"What if it is?"

"Well give him my love when you run into him."

"Sure will," he said.

We rode up to Hijinio's for a couple of drinks.

"Kid what you want to hang around here for?" Hijinio asked.

"Why? You scared?" asked the Kid jokingly.

"Sure," said Hijinio.

"You and me both," said the Kid.

"Listen to him," said Hijinio, showing his teeth in a smile. There was nothing special about Hijinio except that he looked a lot like some of the Indians I had seen around Ensenada. His face was shaped like an egg, the widest part being at the cheekbones, and his chin and forehead were narrow. He had a pleasant dark face with good eyes and a powerful nose, a soft mouth and a wiry scraggly mustache which grew downward. He was a middle-sized fellow, a little taller than the Kid, and wiry.

"How's everything?" asked the Kid.

"Good good," said Hijinio.

"The wife?"

"Good."

"Everything's good," said the Kid. "Been playing any poker lately?"

"Not much."

"Why not?"

"Waiting for you to come back. I knew you'd be back. How could you stay away and miss your old compadre Hijinio Gonzales?"

"Sure," said the Kid. "Let's play."

Hijinio brought out the cards and we played awhile. Hijinio was the richest man on the Punta, it was said. He had inherited land in the hills, cattle, and the adobes on the head. He and the Kid were good friends. As you know, it was in Hijinio's adobe that the Kid got killed.

This adobe was long and had a portico and several rooms, all facing the cove. The easternmost room was Hijinio's and the others were used by members of his family. His own room was square, with a dirt floor. It had several small windows with glass panes, a fireplace, a bureau, a brass bedstead in a corner and a couple of chairs. The door was on the cove side. When you entered, you saw the bed on the right corner farthest from you. It was in that bed that Hijinio lay when the fatal shot was fired. On the left were the fireplace and bureau. The Kid fell just in front of the bureau. Some people said it was Gonzales' fault the Kid got killed, but that is not true. Hijinio knew nothing of what was coming and he himself almost got killed that night.

We got a little drunk and Harvey set to singing some sailor songs he had picked up around Monterey. He was high, the way he had been all the way to old Mex and back, and I wondered again what made him like that. He got up and did a couple of jigs and the Kid began clapping his hands and stomping his feet. I guess Harvey thought he was doing a fandango. Then we all started hopping around but none of us were as good as Harvey.

I liked old Harvey a lot. He was a fellow you could count on to the end and he wasn't the kind that got loose-jawed the minute he had a couple of drinks inside him. He was my boy. He was handsome in his own way, although his face had a hatchet look about it. But I liked the set of his mouth and the clear speckles of his brown eyes and the thinness of his nose and his way of doing things. He was an independent cuss and although he wasn't the world's greatest gunfighter I had a lot of respect for him and so did the Kid.

The Kid took the bottle and had himself a couple of long swigs, saying "Kiss me baby" after each one, and then we danced some more and then I said, "Well let's get moving. How about it?" and we mounted our horses and rode down the trail under the crazy cypresses hanging with moss, down through the meadows and under the pines and past the plaza and out to the mission road. The moon was large and bright that night.

When we were about a hundred yards from the mission road, which was an old dirt road running roughly north and south past the Punta, we approached a big bunch of mesquite on the right. We were riding single file, the Kid in front and Harvey behind him. Suddenly the Kid swung his horse around and came back to where I was, asking for the makings. I handed him tobacco and paper and we continued, Harvey now in front and the Kid behind me.

Then, as we got close to the bunch of mesquite, a shot suddenly rang out from it, together with shouts. I saw the orange burst from the muzzle and wheeled my horse, the Kid wheeling too, and the Kid and I hightailed it back toward the pines, lying low on the horses and shooting at the heap of mesquite. It was then we heard Harvey screaming in a way we knew he had been killed. He had started out after us but now he slowly turned his horse and rode slowly toward the mesquite, facing a small posse that was coming out of the ambush, and saying,

"Don't shoot any more Dad. I'm killed."

Longworth also knew, from those mortal screams, that Harvey was done for, but he was taking no chances.

"Throw your hands up Harvey," he said, covering him with his forty-five.

"I'm killed Dad."

"Throw your hands up. I'm not going to give you a chance to kill me."

"I can't. Don't shoot. I'm dying fellows."

"Take your medicine Harvey," said José Carlyle calmly.

"God damn you," Harvey said, reeling in his saddle. "Which of you boys killed me?"

"I did," Longworth said.

"Take your medicine," said José Carlyle.

"Throw up your hands," said Dad.

"I can't," said Harvey and began to scream again.

Andy Webb walked toward Harvey's horse, meaning to get hold of the reins.

"Watch him Andy," warned Dad. "He's killed all right but he might try for revenge. He can pull a trigger yet."

"I can't," gasped Harvey.

"Watch him," Dad said.

"God damn you," gasped Harvey, almost falling off his horse.

"You're not going to get a chance to kill me Harvey boy," said Longworth.

"Take your medicine," said José Carlyle.

"Get me off this horse," begged Harvey. "For God's sake let me die easy."

They held their guns down on him and went up to him and took his gun out of its holster and his rifle out of its scabbard and lifted him off his horse and laid him down beside the road. They examined him and found that he was shot through the left side, just below the heart. He lay on his back, silent, staring at the stars and breathing heavily. A pool of blood formed beside his left shoulder.

"You killed the wrong fellow?" asked Webb.

"I was sure it was the Kid," Longworth said.

"What's the difference?" José Carlyle said.

"I was sure it was the Kid," Dad said. "I could have sworn it was."

"Who's this fellow?" asked Webb.

"Harvey French," said Dad. "Harvey I'm sorry I killed you," he said.

Harvey blinked his eyes.

"Won't be long now," said José Carlyle.

"Why don't you shut your face?" said Dad angrily.

"I didn't say anything," said José Carlyle.

"No you never do."

"All right Dad all right."

"It's not your fault," said one of the men. "You were doing your duty."

"I was just so sure it was the Kid," said Dad.

"Any reward out for this fellow?" asked Webb.

"No."

"Too bad. You suppose that was the Kid that got away?"

"I don't know," said Dad. "I suppose he's down in old Mex."

"Why don't we go after them?"

Dad eyed Webb ironically. "Webb," he said. "You know where we are?"

"No."

"The Punta. You've heard of it I see. You know what the Kid means to them? They're mostly greasers and Indians in there. If he's in there—"

"Well let's get going," said one of the men.

Dad knelt down. "Harvey," he said, "was that the Kid who got away? Who was with you Harvey? Can you hear me?"

"You killed me," said Harvey slowly.

"Was that the Kid?" asked Dad.

"The Kid's in Mehico," said Harvey.

"You sure?" asked Dad.

"Everybody knows it but you."

"He's lying," José Carlyle said.

"Tell me the truth. You're dying. You've got nothing to lose," Dad said.

"The Kid's in Mehico," said Harvey.

"Well let's get out of here," said Dad, standing up.

"Don't leave me fellows," begged Harvey. "I don't want to die alone."

"If we hang around here much longer—" Dad said.

"Why don't you finish the job?" said Harvey bitterly. "If you were a friend of mine you'd put me out of my misery."

"I'm no friend of yours but I'm sorry I killed you."

"You've killed an innocent man," said Harvey. "May you rot in hell."

José Carlyle pulled out his gun and went over to Harvey and said, "You want me to finish it?"

Harvey looked frightened and said, "Don't! Don't shoot any more! For God's sake I'm killed already!"

Longworth stepped over to José Carlyle and jerked the gun out of his hand.

"I was only kidding," said José Carlyle.

Longworth stuck the gun's muzzle against José Carlyle's stomach and cocked the hammer. José Carlyle's face went white.

"Don't do that Dad," he said whiningly.

"I'm only kidding," Dad said angrily.

He knelt down beside Harvey.

"Harvey you're dying," he said. "The game's over for you. Tell us where the Kid is. There's no harm in telling. You're dying."

"Fuck you," said Harvey and turned his head away.

They slung Harvey face down over his saddle, slapped the horse's rump and rode away. The horse brought Harvey up to the cypress head. The Kid and I were outside the Kid's adobe, waiting for trouble. We saw that Harvey was still alive and we carried him into the adobe and laid him on the bunk. Harvey opened his eyes and saw us. He smiled.

"They're gone away," he said. "They've killed me."

"That's too bad," said the Kid.

"I told them you were in Mehico."

"Who killed you?"

"Dad."

The Kid made a wry face.

"It was lucky for you you went back for the makings," Harvey said.

"You're a good boy," said the Kid.

"I'm glad I don't have to die alone," Harvey said.

"You in pain?" I asked.

"Some," said Harvey. "Hi Doc."

"Hi Harvey."

"I'll be taking me a trip tonight."

"Have a drink," said the Kid.

Harvey gulped the whiskey and coughed, then seemed to fall asleep. I'm going to take off soon, he was thinking. I've always thought it would be like a great white sheet of silk and I would have to walk, a long way over it and would sink down to my thighs in it and before getting lost in it I would look down behind me and down below I would see the earth spinning, with cobwebs all over it and fat spiders sitting on it.

I lit a couple of tallow candles and the Kid and I sat down to a game of stud.

"I hear he hails from Wisconsin," I said.

The Kid shook his head to say he didn't know.

"He wasn't bad with a horse," I said, "but never very good with a gun. I tried to teach him but he just didn't have the knack of it. A fellow like that is bound to get himself killed before he's twenty-five. He would have made somebody a good foreman though."

"He just picked the wrong trade that's all," said the Kid, studying his cards.

"He was sure mighty handy with a branding iron."

I'm going to take off soon, Harvey was thinking. I used to have a horse when I was a kid. I was a great rider when I was fifteen. Fifteen is the best time in a fellow's life. I've been going downhill ever since.

He felt a cold hand touch him but he did not bother to open his eyes to see whose it was.

"He's still alive," I said.

"Harvey," a voice said.

Thinking carefully, Harvey was able to decide it was the Kid's but he was too tired to answer.

"I think he's dead," someone said.

Someone felt his wrist.

"No he's still alive," another voice said.

"Come on back and play," said the Kid. "He'll die soon enough."

Why the hell did I get mixed up in all this? Harvey was thinking. Maybe I can get somebody to figure it out. Harvey your time is short you know that?

Suddenly he screamed and we looked up from our game and watched him. He screamed again and then we heard the rattle in his throat. He jerked twice and was still.

"Well that's that," said the Kid. "Let's get him buried. I reckon they'll want to have a wake."

"Good old Harvey," I said.

The natives had a wake for Harvey in the barn and Jesús Garcia buried him that night. The Kid and I spent the night in our adobes in the cypress head. Harvey's killing had caused quite a commotion on the Punta, some of the natives thinking it was the Kid who had been killed. Nika knew now for sure that if the Kid hung around the Punta much longer he would find himself a bullet the way Harvey had and the more she thought about this the more she felt that the Kid was there only because of her and that she would be responsible for his death. Right after Harvey was buried she came over to the Kid's adobe. He was lying on his bunk in his clothes, one tallow candle burning on the small table.

"That could have been you," she said quietly. He had heard her come up the path and into the adobe.

"So what?" he said.

"Poor Harvey," she said.

"A lucky shot," he said. "Lucky for me."

He stood up and set his hands in his back pockets.

"Your luck's going to change if you keep hanging around here," she said.

"What do you know about my luck?" he asked. "My luck's better than ever. Don't you know that?"

"It won't last forever."

"What am I supposed to do—bust out crying?"

"A little crying might do you some good. Aren't you sorry for him?"

He shrugged.

"When your luck gives out that's the end of the game," he said.

"I don't like to hear you talk like that."

"I didn't say it to please you."

"No I know you didn't."

"This what you came to tell me?" he asked.

"No."

"What then?"

She looked at him. "I don't know."

And then she went up to him, very close, watching his eyes intently, waiting for them to tell her something, and he held her shoulders gently and she pressed her cheek against his neck, thinking, I'm married to Miguel, and remembering Miguel lying in his bed, hollow-cheeked, the forehead looking too large, the nose looking thin and pinched, and she thought, I hope he won't die, poor Miguel, and the Kid gripped her shoulders and she watched his eyes again in that intense way, trying to read them, and he kissed her. They said nothing in the dimness of the place, in the earth-smelling place with the madonna on the wall, and as he probed her mouth with his tongue she thought again of Miguel, thinking, Poor Miguel, I hope he won't die.

9

There was no secret about how it happened or who did it. Late the next afternoon, Thursday, Cal and Curly Bill Dedrick and a fellow named Shotgun Smith rode up to the ranch where Modesto worked and called him out front. He went into the yard in front of the corral and asked them what they wanted. His boss was there too. They were liquored up and sweating and laughing to beat the band.

"Hell kid we just want to be sociable," Curly Bill said.

"So you think you're pretty good with that thing on your hip," said Cal.

"I don't want any trouble with you," said Modesto, un-hitching his gunbelt and letting it fall to the ground.

"Come here Modesto I got something for you," said Curly Bill and he jerked his forty-five and shot him.

The ball hit Modesto in the stomach. He staggered, clawing at his gut. The Dedrick boys and Smith thought it was a great joke. Modesto straightened up partly, the blood running out over his fingers.

"The Kid will get you for this," he said quietly.

It was at this point that Shotgun Smith fired a barrel into

Modesto's head. The boy dropped and Curly Bill dismounted and kicked his face with the high heel of his boot. Cal dismounted too, got a large rock and laid it under Modesto's head for a pillow. Then Curly Bill, spotting Modesto's piebald in the corral, roped her, led her close to the boy and shot her in the head. When she lay dead, steaming, the urine running out of her and the blood staining the ground, he got Modesto's hat, which had fallen near the body, and put it under the mare's head.

"You go and tell the Kid about this," said Curly Bill to Modesto's boss. "Tell him this is what he's going to get too."

Francisco Romero crossed himself. As he later said, his blood froze at the horror of it. When they left he saddled up a horse and tore off for the Punta.

I can still see the two of them in front of the Kid's place, the sea behind them, the Kid looking delicate beside the large Romero, his gun thonged around his thigh. He wore dark woolen trousers and a soft white shirt and black boots and Romero bulked large and dusty beside him in his work clothes, gesturing violently, crossing himself, covering his eyes with his hands, trembling and beginning to sob. The Kid stood motionless with his slightly bowed legs, his pink hands resting on his gunbelt. But then his face looked tired and I can see it now, the weariness that came into it, into the eyes and under the eyes and around the nose, the taut weariness of luck going sour, and I reckon from that moment on things were never the same for him, it was that moment that really began the rolling downhill which ended as it could only end, in his own untimely and mysterious death.

I walked over and said, "Trouble?"

"The Dedrick boys have killed Modesto," he said grimly.

We saddled up and rode out to the valley to Francisco Romero's ranch. Modesto lay just as they had left him. The Kid pulled his horse up short a little way from the body, dismounted and walked up quietly. I followed him. Romero stood a way off, crossing himself and sobbing. Glancing at the body, I began to feel sick to my stomach. It is really something what a load of buckshot can do to the human face at close range. You would not see such a sight in a slaughterhouse. Modesto was no longer the young kid we had known but a mess of blood and flesh and bone, all mixed up in a kind of paste and lather, some still oozing, some already dried black and beginning to crack. I turned away, not able to bear it, and accidentally caught a glimpse of the Kid's face. I was shocked by what I saw.

He was rolling a cigarette with a steady hand but his eyes were full of tears and his lips were trembling. It hit me in the stomach to see him like that.

"That Bob," he said.

I knew then that Bob was done for, that the Kid was blaming him for jinxing his luck, but I had done all I could for Bob and it was now too late for me to do any more. Bob had just insisted on bucking his luck and now he would have to take the consequences. Well I wasn't going to lose any sleep over him. I still remembered how he had tried to steal my horses the first time we met and I had no doubt he would have killed me then if I hadn't beaten him to the draw. And maybe the Kid was right—maybe Bob *had* jinxed us all.

That night the Kid and I rode down to Monterey in the fog and went over to the Dedrick house. There were no lights showing. We dismounted. While I covered the Kid from behind an old adobe wall he went up to the door and knocked. No answer. We settled down behind the wall, our Winchester barrels resting on the ledge. At about ten o'clock Curly Bill came along. By then the fog had lifted. He was on foot. I wondered where Cal was.

He was prematurely gray, was lean and tall and wore his hair short. He did not swagger like Lon and wore only one gun, thonged and low down and well forward on his thigh. His upper lip was caved in a little and he wore a wide mustache to hide it. That was all there was to him and that little didn't last long. When he got close to his door the Kid fired twice and dusted him off on both sides, the bullets kicking up dust on his back where they entered and on his chest where they came out. He dropped with a grunt and never knew what hit him. The Kid went over to him and shot him through the head to make sure.

Then we rode over to Shotgun Smith's and waited in a clump of trees near by. There was no light in the adobe. After waiting awhile the Kid went to the door and knocked on it but there was no answer. In about a half hour Shotgun Smith came along, a heavyset fellow with a thick beard and a beaked nose and a smile that twisted to one side. The Kid suddenly stepped out of the shadows and faced him, his right hand hanging by his side. Shotgun recognized him and stopped dead, sucking in air.

"Go on go to shooting," said the Kid quietly.

But Shotgun could not bring himself to reach for his gun. He kept staring at the Kid's right hand. Then he began walking toward the Kid, coming closer and closer, and the Kid said, "Make your play and quit wasting my time."

Shotgun went for his gun but before it was half out the Kid had drilled him through the heart. He went over to Shotgun and shot him through the head too.

There was a fine mist falling when we returned to the Punta. We came to my place, where I made a fire. We were hungry. I rustled up a chunk of meat which I roasted. We had a couple of drinks.

"One to go," the Kid said.

But he never did get that Cal. Cal got out of that country. I understand he was killed in Tombstone a couple of years later.

Of course there was hell to pay with Nika. When she heard of her brother's killing she just went crazy—screaming, kicking—until she had to be held down by some women. She blamed the Kid for it, calling him Modesto's murderer. You'd have thought, the way she carried on, that she had never heard of anybody getting killed before. But some women are like that.

The next afternoon, Friday, July fifteenth, exactly six weeks since the Kid had escaped, the Kid and I rode down to Old

Man Richardson's ranch. Bob was up and about and feeling pretty good. We told him about Harvey. It did not seem to upset him. I suspected from the way he took the news and from the way he was behaving in general that he had made up his mind to take off. I thought: Bob your farting days are over but you don't know it. You should have taken off when I told you. We did not mention the Modesto killing.

Old Man Richardson had received a report from one of his hands that Longworth was going to be in Monterey the next day. It was what the Kid had been waiting for. He instructed the Mexican to ride into town the next morning and give Longworth a message. What that message was I never did find out.

"What are you telling Dad?" I asked.

"That I'm back."

"That all?"

The Kid laughed.

"What else?" I asked.

"You want to know too much," he said. "You'll find out."

"So will Dad."

"You bet," he said, grinning.

The Kid did some snap shooting and then went off to have a talk with Old Man Richardson. When he returned Bob suggested we go off hunting but the Kid said he wanted to rustle some steers over at Rancho Canada Honda and asked us to come along with him. I said I couldn't because my right shoulder, which had been shot up a couple of years back, was acting up and that the pain was bad and that I would have to booze up to kill it. I actually felt some pain in my shoulder but it was not that bad. I saw that the Kid understood and that Bob didn't. They rode off.

Old Man Richardson and I sat around outside, talking. It was very hot. We had been having some good sunsets and on this day we sat and watched one. The sky was empty except for a thin cloud on the right, with a tip like an arrowhead, and the top of this cloud was violet and the bottom pink. The colors kept changing all the time and under them the ocean was glassy and green and seemed to give off its own light. The country on the right was so dark you could make out no details except for some trees showing up against the neat blue sky.

We sat there and talked and the long cloud turned gray and the shadows and silhouettes got deeper and the ocean looked like a huge abalone shell with the mother-of-pearl side facing the sky. There was a smell of seaweed in the air and the breakers looked like burning oil. Everything turned gloomy and blue and the trees stuck out black against the ocean light.

The Kid returned alone, without any steers. I knew he had killed Bob. I made up my mind to say nothing about it. We slept together in a shack behind the barn. In the early part of the night I awoke to hear him talking in his sleep. It sounded like, "Take your medicine Bob." Then he began to cuss and toss. I went over to him. It was a very hot night and he was sweating heavily. He was sleeping in his pants and socks, without a blanket. Several times he groaned as if he was being tortured and muttered what sounded like, "Take your medicine Bob." I shook him and he opened his eyes.

"Easy Kid," I said. I lit a candle. We sat drinking whiskey and saying nothing. His face looked thin and tired and old. I was sure then that he would never leave that country, that he would be buried there.

We went to sleep after a while and I had a dream. In the middle of it I opened my eyes. I could see nothing but I felt uncomfortable. I wondered what was wrong, if a spider had run across my face or if a scorpion had scuttled on the floor. Then I saw the Kid standing there and I could not believe my eyes.

He was standing there slightly crouched, like a cat waiting to spring, and by the bright moonlight drifting in from the doorway I caught the shine of his blond hair and the glint of his blond stubble. I saw his wiry muscular chest, with the blond hair glinting in the bluish light. He had a gun in his hand, pointing it at me.

I just lay there, looking at him, not even thinking of reaching for my gun under the pillow, and waiting for the bullet which would end the suspense. I wondered in a flash if the real reason he had killed Bob was that he suspected him of having something to do with Nika, and I wondered if Bob had told him about Nika and me. I wanted him to say something but he didn't. I kept watching his eyes, knowing that I had to hold them as long as possible. Ordinarily, if I had a chance for my life, I would have watched his right hand.

He was rolling down that well-known street all right. He was tired, deathly tired. When I had first met him he was like a boy, believing the bullet hadn't been made that had his number on it. His face was tight and clean, his whoops loud and frequent. But that seemed very long ago. I thought: Doc you're done for, the game's over. Take your medicine. But then I saw something and my heart jumped, but I was not sure what I had seen.

He seemed to have been standing there like that for years. The memory of it seemed to have been branded into my mind: the Kid crouching like that, with his gun pointing at me and my heart afraid to beat for fear it would set the trigger off, my eyes glued to his eyes, and he just standing there, legs apart, and pointing that forty-four at me.

And then I caught the flash of that thing again, the thing in my mind, and I thought: *he's not all there.* By this I meant that his attention, or the main part of it, was somewhere else, somewhere he himself didn't know where. I pinned my hope on it. It was what saved me, I think. Suddenly I got tired of the whole thing.

"Go on. Get it over with," I said, sitting up.

He sat down on an old chair, looking at his feet. He offered me the gun, butt first, meaning for me to shoot him. I shook my head to say I wouldn't. He began to sob. So you see he had really changed.

It was still early—about nine o'clock. I didn't want to sleep on that ranch any more that night. I suggested we go over to the Punta. He liked the idea. There was a light on in Old Man Richardson's house. We told him we were leaving.

"Take it easy boys," he said, waving.

"Sure," I said and we rode off.

As we rode along I saw by the bright moonlight how tired

the Kid's face was. There was a funny tired expression in his eyes and I realized now I had seen it for some time. He was just plumb tired of being on his guard, I reckon. I was tired in that way too. Whenever we used to sit down to a meal it was never side by side but around the fire, facing each other. That was the way we always ate or sat around, so we could see behind each other's backs and guard against being surprised. When we ate, our rifles were always across our laps or lying handy close by. It was always like that. Eating is very dangerous when you are being hunted.

In the old days it had been fun to live like that, but now we were tired. The Kid looked so tired I was greatly surprised. The life of being always hunted was really changing him. And changing me too, I had no doubt.

We went up to the cypress head and went to sleep, the Kid in his adobe and I in mine. And the craziest part of it all is that around midnight Nika, who had not known that we had gone back to the ranch, left her own place, with Miguel asleep, and went to the Kid's and without a word got into bed with him. You figure that one out if you can. I heard them whispering. I don't know what they were talking about. The sound got twisted on the way between the two adobes and there was always the noise of the cove. But I knew it was Nika all right and I wished I had myself a woman too for a change.

Well, that's about the end of this story. You know the end as well as I do. Given the circumstances, how could it have been any different?

*

There was this fellow Brazil, a drunken old geezer, who was getting himself handouts over in Salinas, and Whitey Pearce, the same fellow that shot Dad Longworth in the back of the head a couple of years later, and had himself a hayloft there, would let Brazil sleep in it now and then. On Friday afternoon, the fifteenth, when Whitey thought Brazil was asleep he and his brother Jim were talking about the Kid in that barn and about how the Kid was back in those parts and about how they would ride over to see him in a day or two and make some business propositions to him. Brazil was not asleep. Drunk as he was he knew he had himself an interesting piece of information. He went out to hunt up Longworth's new deputy, a fellow out of Texas by the name of Andy Webb.

He was a damned old coot, this Brazil, a dry tall stoop-shouldered man with a small dry mouth, black hair combed back and a reddish vandyke streaked with gray. He wore some old black pants somebody had given him, some broken-down boots, and a brown shirt with the sleeves torn off, showing his flabby pale arms, and he went squinting around, unshaven, down the bright dirt streets, and in the saloon next to Johnson's Hotel he found Webb and said, "May I see you a minute Mr Webb? I got something I want to talk to you about."

Webb, who was standing at the bar, looked at this fellow and pursed his small mouth. He knew that Brazil was "addicted to habits of dissipation," as he liked to put it, but that he was "a man of good principles on the side of law and order." They went outside and Brazil told him what he had overheard.

"Hell the Kid's in old Mex," growled Webb, spitting off to one side.

But he reached into his pocket and gave Brazil a three-dollar gold piece.

"You know what'll happen to me if they found out I told you," said Brazil.

Webb nodded and walked away.

"Goodbye Mr Webb," said Brazil.

But Webb did not seem to have heard.

The fact is I never did cotton to this fellow Webb and I'll tell you why. He *did* get married later on and so he did find at least somebody who liked him, although even that's not necessarily so, because so many women will marry a fellow for so many reasons and anyhow I've noticed that the strangest birds will find birds of a feather.

I ran into him many years later over in Fresno and he was a banker by then and to look at him you'd never have believed he had once been a cowhand and a deputy. He wore tight striped trousers and a morning coat, mind you, and a black bowler and a hard collar and if I hadn't recognized Andy Webb I'd have sworn I was looking at a fancy embalmer. There he was in a swelterpot like Fresno and wearing the hard collar and the coat.

He had changed, all right. His once dark and gaunt face was now sallow and pouchy and he didn't walk like a cowhand any more but straight and stiff, as though he'd had the kinks and curves taken out of his legs by some high-classed doctor, and when I asked him if he ever rode saddle any more he smiled and said, "Regrettably not". Regrettably my foot: he had never talked like that in the old days.

I could see he was as fascinated with me as I was with him and I wondered what I looked like—but I knew what I looked like, I hadn't changed much with the years and if I was a funny sight to some people at least it was because I had never turned coat, you might say. I had money then too— most of us old fellows who had managed to stay alive also had managed to get hold of some money—and my hair was white and long, coming down almost to my shoulders, and I wore a long white goatee and black clothes of the kind we had used to wear in the Kid's day on going into town, and a black wide-brimmed Stetson and shiny black high-heeled boots. It was what I'd been wearing all along in those years and I had no meaning behind it, I just felt comfortable in them and it was like old times. Besides which, it was still California, and the place hadn't changed that much. But the bowler and the hard collar—imagine a fellow wearing those things in a place like Fresno.

"Andy," I says, meaning to be polite, "I guess we've both changed a bit."

"We sure have," he says, looking me up and down.

"And how've you been?" says I.

"Very fine thank you," he says, and never once during that meeting did he mention my name, so that after a while I suspected he couldn't remember who I was.

"Me too," I says. "Very fine."

And after a little more chitchat we broke away. There was just lots of no good in that fellow. He had always looked like an embalmer, all the way back, with that long narrow dark face and those large owl eyes. You never knew exactly where he had come from or where he was heading and it made you kind of mad. Not that you expected to know much about a fellow in those days. There were lots of us who wouldn't have given you our right names or told you much of anything about ourselves even if you had asked, and if you had insisted we might have given you a little taste of lead for your trouble. But Webb was the sort of fellow you just felt you had a right to know something about, and yet there wasn't anyone I met back in that time that ever knew much about him. He was unmarried as far as we knew and a pretty good shot, a fair cowhand, a quiet fellow who liked to do an honest job—and that was about all we knew about him. But even then I didn't like him much. He was not a fellow to drink much or to talk much or to go with women so as you'd know about it, and besides which he was a deputy—although, come to think of it, that was all he must have been good for: a deputy or a banker.

He was a strange-looking bird too, in addition to being one. He had a body like the letter I—that was all there was to him: a long loose body with a gooseneck and a big adam's apple and when he laughed it was not a good laugh but a series of coughs and honks. And that wasn't all, either. Every time he would laugh—which was seldom—his small mouth would open like a widening hole and show his square yellow teeth, but mostly you would notice his gums, because his mouth was built up and down and stretched up and down under his nose when he laughed. And then there would come out those coughs and snickers and hiccups and honks, and you would wonder what he was really thinking about, and what sort of juice he had inside of him, and how come some fellow hadn't shot him full of holes long since. I didn't know him too well in those days but I met him in one place or another after the Kid's death and heard about all I wanted to hear about him. He claimed to be only twenty-three at the time the Kid was killed but he looked about ten years older. His hair was gray on the sides of his head and his eyes were gaunt and dark-rimmed, with scaly-looking lids. He talked in a high voice like a whine and I just didn't care for the man.

Later that afternoon when Longworth rode into town Webb told him what Brazil had heard. Dad put little stock in it.

"Still," he said, "Whitey ought to know. He's an old friend of the Kid's. Maybe Harvey did give us a bum steer. Maybe we ran onto the Kid that night. No harm in snooping around. How about that?"

"It's all right by me," said Webb.

"Well Andy if it's all right by you we'll just do this little thing."

"You're a great little kidder aren't you Dad?"

"Hell boy I was born with a joke in my mouth," said Dad.

And so that night Longworth, Webb and José Carlyle rode out of Salinas in the direction of Santa Cruz to throw people off their scent, then turned south across the hills and headed for the Punta. It was about eleven o'clock when they reached the Punta. They picketed their horses in a grove of pines near the plaza, then hid out behind an old wall and watched the plaza to see if the Kid was stirring about. But in about a half hour they gave it up and sneaked up to the cypress head to see what they could find up there. They hid out there, watching, but saw and heard nothing. They did not know that the Kid had a place up there and were not even sure that he was very friendly with Hijinio. They went up there because it was the only other settlement on the Punta. Longworth whispered that it was his opinion they were on a cold trail and that he had thought so all along. He proposed they leave the Punta at once and without letting anyone know they had been there in search of the Kid. Then he said, "But wait. I'll just drop in on Gonzales and see what he knows." And he went into Hijinio's room, leaving the two deputies squatting on the porch under the long portico, and began to rouse Gonzales gently, putting his hand over Gonzales' mouth.

Meanwhile I was sleeping, half drunk, in my own place, unaware of any danger, and the Kid got up, restless and hungry, woke Nika and told her he wanted something to eat. She said there was a fresh-killed yearling over by the barn, which Jesús Garcia had killed that evening. You could not hear their voices very far because of the noise of the water in the cove. And so he got a long knife and, pulling on his trousers and getting hold of his forty-four, went out in his stockinged feet to cut himself a chunk of meat.

If they had only talked louder and waked me. Or if he had only come and pushed my shoulder as he often did. For then I might have gone with him or I might have gone to fetch the meat for him, seeing as how he was only half awake, still very drowsy from loving that Nika. If I had gone they would not have killed me, or if they had tried to I would have maybe killed one or more of them. But that would be a different story and everybody knows it didn't turn out that way. The Kid always used to say that if a bullet has your number on it there is nothing you can do to dodge it, and he was going out now to meet his bullet and there I was asleep, and me his compadre too.

There was this bright moonlight outside and to appreciate how bright it was you have to know how it can be out there on the Punta in a full moon, the light falling on the trails and on the pine and cedar and cypress tags and hanging on the Spaniard's beard and flashing up from the ocean and flashing on the gnarled cypress trunks and arms and fingers and lighting up the air so to speak and bringing the cries and barks and grunts of the seawolves onto the land with it and casting the deep shadows. You'd think that with that light the Kid would have seen enough to protect himself but the thing was I think that it kind of blinded him, making that head seem like a dream. It was on nights like that, the natives used to say, that it was best to kill a man, but I think it would have been all right for him if he hadn't just loved that damned Nika and gotten up from sleep hungry and gone off in his stockinged feet for a chunk of meat.

He carried the knife in his right hand, where his sixshooter ought to have been, and the gun in his left. He took the trail which went past Hijinio's to the barn and when he was half-way there he spotted the two dark figures squatting on the porch, looking as if they were whittling something. That stopped him, for he wondered who these fellows were, sitting there this time of night on Hijinio's porch. Going to the barn would put his back to them. Returning to his place would do the same. He could have gone off into the brush but he was too tired to think of that. He could have hailed them but since they hadn't seen him he didn't want to do that. And so he decided to go into Hijinio's place, covering them with the forty-four. He didn't want to get caught out in the open like that. Once he was inside Hijinio's he could make them come and get him, if that was what they wanted, and once inside there he could find out from Hijinio who these fellows were, sitting on his porch.

He didn't want to hurt Hijinio or his friends but if these fellows were out to kill him and if Hijinio knew about it and was friendly to them and let them sit out there on his porch, in the moonlight, partly in shadow, looking as if they were whittling something, then he would kill Hijinio first and get that over with and then he would give his attention to the two fellows. For that was the kind of hombre the Kid was, very businesslike and liking to keep everything neat where his life and death were concerned.

It was Webb who saw him first. The figure he saw was not what he had in mind for the Kid. He had never seen the Kid and he thought this was a sheepherder from the hills who was currently staying with Gonzales. He saw a slight but lithe man approaching him, a rather youthful man, bare-headed, in stockinged feet, naked to the hips, close-cropped on the head, one hand fumbling with the buttons of his trousers while it carried something which flashed in the moonlight, the other holding what looked like a long knife. Hoping to get some information from him, Webb stood up and hailed him softly, upon which the Kid thrust out his right arm and Webb saw that he was covered. José Carlyle immediately straightened up but, being behind Webb, did not get a good look at the Kid. But José Carlyle also had never seen him.

If either of the deputies had realized he was facing the Kid's forty-four he might have flinched and then, perhaps, the Kid would have shot and thus saved himself. But they did not flinch and the Kid held his fire, although he had them well covered.

"Take it easy hombre we're not going to hurt you," Webb said softly, stepping forward.

"Quién es?" whispered the Kid, meaning "Who is it?" And he backed away. "Quién es?"

Again Webb stepped forward and it's a mystery why the Kid didn't shoot him. But he probably thought Webb was a friend of Hijinio's or maybe even a relative.

"Quién es?" he whispered again, and backed into the doorway of Hijinio's room, where he paused, his body concealed by the thick wall. Peering out at Webb, he asked again, "Quién es?"

By this time Webb was beginning to feel a fluttering inside his stomach and he froze, not wishing to push his luck any further. José Carlyle froze with him. And then the Kid darted into the adobe, where Longworth was squatting in the dark beside the head of Hijinio's bed, having been talking in whispers with Hijinio, whom he had awakened.

Nobody was more surprised than Longworth by what happened next. He had heard a voice saying "Quién es?" several times and then a figure, with the moonlight behind it, sprang into the room, bare-headed and apparently bare-footed, and came over to the bed, almost touching him but not seeing him crouching there, and whispered,

"Hijinio! Who are those fellows outside?"

Hijinio didn't answer and the Kid said again, "Hijinio! Who are they?"

And then Longworth, who had thought for a moment that it might be Hijinio's brother-in-law, Ignacio Romero, knew by the voice that it was the Kid and he slowly made a move to reach for his gun, trying to look very small and dark there in the corner beside the bed.

The Kid felt something moving there and covered the crouching figure with his gun, retreating rapidly across the room and crying, "Quién es? Quién es?" as if it was the devil himself.

And then Longworth drew and fired and threw his body to the left and fired again from close to the floor, lighting up the room, and sprang up and ran outside and pressed himself against the wall at the side of the door, looking pale in the moonlight.

The Kid probably never knew what hit him. Coming out of the moonlight into that dark room, he was aware only of darkness and of his own danger and of how tired he was and of how tired of loving he was and of how he would have to leave that country he liked, the heads, meadows, coves, beaches, fog, hills, sun, ocean, seawolves, trees, and of how he would have to get himself down to old Mex. And then the red flame sprang at him and the forty-five ball crashed into his chest and it was as though a tree had hit him trunk first and then he heard the roar like the roar of the sea and found himself face down on the dirt floor, wondering how he had got there, and he was gasping and gurgling, and he said faintly, "Mother. Help me. I'm strangling."

When the Kid darted into Hijinio's adobe and Webb felt the fluttering inside his stomach Webb did not know what to do. He peered into the doorway but could make out nothing. Then he saw the flames and staggered back out of the way, shoving against José Carlyle and bruising José's left side. He thought he had heard three shots but Dad's second shot had gone wild and ricocheted off a wall. José Carlyle grunted and flattened himself against the house. Both men drew their guns and waited, wondering if Dad was dead.

Then Dad rushed out. They heard groans and gasps and gurgling inside and then the sounds stopped. Webb moved toward the door, sixshooter ready, then Hijinio, running from his bed with the bedclothes dragging after him, crashed into him and Webb threw down on him and would have shot him if Dad hadn't knocked the gun down and cried, "Don't! It's Gonzales!"

By this time Dad was away from the wall, but still pale and breathing hard, and they all stood away from the doorway and listened. But there was no sound inside.

"That was the Kid that came in onto me," whispered Dad. "I think I got him."

Webb, remembering the half-naked figure that looked like a sheepherder and that had spoken Spanish, said, "Dad I think you've shot the wrong man."

"I wouldn't mistake his voice," said Longworth. "I'd know his voice."

"I hope so," Webb said.

And there was I, asleep when all this happened. When I heard the shots I jumped up, grabbed my gun from under my pillow and ran into the Kid's place. Nika lay naked on the bed. I ran out and ran towards Hijinio's in my pants and bare feet (I had been sleeping in my pants), but when I saw them standing out there I knew I could not kill them all before they killed me, and anyhow I was still half asleep and half drunk and I was not sure what had happened or who those men were, for the moonlight was playing tricks, and so I ran back into the Kid's place and stood staring at Nika.

She must have been twenty-three at the time but her body was still good, tight and brown, with the black hair, and her breasts not bad, although they were getting hangy. I went up to her and touched her shoulder but she was drunk and hard asleep. I smelled the rotgut she had been drinking and saw the sweat of sleep between her breasts and I thought, "Jesus I'd like to give you a tumble baby" and then went back to my place and sat down and tried to think this thing out.

Meanwhile nobody had any hankering to go inside Hijinio's place to see who was in there and if he was dead.

"What do you think Gonzales? Is it the Kid?" whispered José Carlyle.

"It's the Kid," said Hijinio.

"What did I tell you?" whispered Longworth.

Dad had some sulphur matches. He lit one and threw it inside the adobe, craning for a look, but it sputtered and went out. He lit a couple of others and threw them in but they went out before he or the others could get a good look.

"It could have been him or me," whispered Longworth, "but this is my night."

"The night's not over yet," said Hijinio.

"What do you mean by that?"

"Nothing. What you think I mean?"

"Well if you mean nothing get us a light."

"You kidding?"

Dad jabbed his forty-five into Hijinio's side, making Hijinio double up. "You son of a bitch get us a light."

"Dad—" Hijinio began.

Dad cocked his gun, his lips drawing back in a snarl.

"I'll get it," said Hijinio and he walked down toward his mother's room at the end of the portico.

"Take it easy Dad," said Webb.

Dad threw down on him and said, "You want to get yours too?"

Webb looked hard at him and said, "One of these days someone's going to give it to you Longworth."

"You call me Dad you son of a bitch."

"Easy boys," said José Carlyle.

Hijinio returned with a candle, which, without a glance at Longworth, he lit and placed on the window sill of his room. Peering in, they saw a figure lying stretched out on the floor face down. They went in, covering it with their guns. Longworth bent down and rolled the body over, then stood up and said softly, "Boys the Kid is dead."

There was a sixshooter in the Kid's right hand and a long knife lying beside his left. Longworth's ball had struck him just above the heart, a good shot. It had left a neat hole where it had entered, with only a trickle of blood, but had torn a large hole in his back.

"Damned good shot," said Webb.

"Lucky," said Dad.

"No."

"I guess I talked out of turn. Sorry."

"That's all right," said Webb.

Hijinio stood near the bed. Dad went over to him and stuck out his hand but Hijinio wouldn't shake. Dad sat down on the bed with a sigh and wiped his forehead with his sleeve. Then he went to study the body again.

At this point Francesca ran in, knelt over the body, then

suddenly faced Longworth and cried, "You pisspot you! You shot him in the dark!"

Dad made a wry face and said nothing. They went outside, leaving Francesca with the body.

"How many shots did you fire?" asked Webb.

"Two," said Dad.

"In that case the Kid must have fired. I heard three."

They examined the Kid's gun, which Dad had brought out, and found that it contained five cartridges and one shell, the hammer resting on the shell. But the shell looked as if it had been fired some time before, and when they looked around for its bullet mark later they couldn't find it in the room.

At this point I walked up, without my gun. I went into the room and stared at the body. Francesca paid no attention to me. She just knelt there, weeping. I went outside.

"Who did it?" I asked.

"I did," said Dad. "It was him or me. He walked in onto me."

"You shot him in the dark."

"What would you have done in my place?"

"I'm not in your place. Remember?"

"Who's this bird?" asked Webb.

"Doc Baker."

"Oh so you're the tough boy," said Webb. "Should we take him in?"

"No," said Dad. "We can always get him if we want him."

"That's right," I said. "Any time you want me just send me your calling card."

"That's just what I mean," said Dad.

I started to leave.

"Where you going?" Webb said.

I spat between his feet and turned my back on him and walked away.

Well Kid, I thought, you can have yourself a long rest now. And then I thought, As for you Doc, you'd better think of shoving off tomorrow. Montana, Arizona, anywhere. You need a fresh start.

I went to the Kid's adobe. Nika lay just as I had left her, on her back. I thought, It's a funny thing. He's just got through being with her and now he's in Hijinio's place, with those fellows hanging around.

"Nika," I said.

She opened her eyes.

"He's dead," I said.

I saw that she knew.

"What are you going to do about it?" she asked quietly.

"Aren't you surprised?" I said.

"What are you going to do about it?" she asked.

"There's not a damned thing I *can* do," I said. I wondered how she knew. Somebody must have told her.

She said nothing. She just lay there naked in the heat.

"Nika,' I said. "You ought to cover yourself."

She closed her eyes and tears came from under the lids but she made no sound and her face did not seem to move.

"It's a hell of a thing," I said.

I wanted to get out of that room or else to get on the bed

with her and forget that night's business and the crazy moonlight outside.

"You just stand there," she said.

"There's nothing I can do," I said, thinking now of Montana.

"Get out of here," she said. "You dog."

"If that's how you feel," I said.

I went back to Hijinio's under those crazy cypresses with
the thrust-out fingers and the Spaniard's beard and the red
soft growth like antler's fur burning the undersides, and I
stared at the thin trail and the crumbling shells of the mound
and at the narrow strip of surf-beaten moonlit water and at
the great whited rock with the squatting gulls and cormorants. The tallow candle still burned in the window sill but
when I went inside I saw the Kid was not there. I looked
down at where he had fallen. There was blood on the floor.
The knife and gun were gone too. It was a hell of a thing, me
his compadre just standing there in the hot room in my bare
feet on the dirt floor and feeling tired and sleepy and a little
drunk. I wished then I had stopped off in my place for another
couple of drinks.

I stood in the doorway and looked around outside and saw
lights in the barn and figured they had carried him there, so
I went there to get another look at him. Remembering I was
bare-footed, I stuck to the middle of the trail and tried not to
brush up against the poison oak, which I could see shining in
the moonlight. I stumped my toe against a rock and then cut
my left foot on a shell. What was I doing without my gun just
because Longworth and his deputies were around? I thought

about this but couldn't come to any decision and so I just kept going toward the barn. I figure now sometimes that a man with guts and a sixshooter and rifle could have finished those three off and I wonder why I didn't do it. But I know why, only that's not part of this story.

They were standing on the right of the barn, against an adobe in the shadow of a large pine, their guns in their scabbards and their hands on their butts. They weren't any too happy standing there, thinking they'd be jumped any minute, and I wondered why they didn't light out, but then it occurred to me that Dad would want an inquest to make everything legal. He was probably waiting for the wake to end so he could have the inquest afterward. They must have been tired and sleepy and itching to go back to town. It wasn't the first man Dad had killed and I had heard he didn't mind letting a fellow lie to rot, without a thought about an inquest, but this one was different, this one had friends who would be waiting to blow Dad's head off from an ambush and if enough feeling got stirred up he might even get himself strung up, his big feet kicking at the state of California. Besides, his reputation was at stake. It was up to him to prove he had killed the Kid fair and in the line of duty. It was always healthy in such circumstances to have an inquest quick and over with and on the record, so some jokers couldn't later indict you for something you had had to do, jokers who were after your scalp, say when some time had passed and maybe with a new set of fellows in office.

When they saw me they stirred but they did not pull down

on me. They weren't too eager to have a shot fired now, being afraid that if one man fired a lot of others would come piling in and finish them off. They were playing it soft now, hanging around for a purpose and hating it and expecting to be attacked any minute. I give them credit for that night's work. Of course it was only Longworth who had to stick it out. The other two could have moseyed off, but if they had they would have been through in that country.

I entered the barn and saw the women were dressing the Kid. They had laid him out on a workbench and I could see that he had cooled off and was stiffening. It was funny to think of him as cold on that hot night. You wouldn't find more than a couple of nights a year like that on the Punta and it had to be one of them the Kid was killed on. The barn was lit by a few tallow candles. When Francesca saw me she gave me a hard look and I knew she hated me now but I had my own worries just then and I didn't give a damn for her anyhow, knowing there was nothing I could do unless I was a better or a different man from what I was, and anyway I would have to be leaving soon and it would be no great weight for me to carry, that look she gave me. I knew what she was thinking and I couldn't say I blamed her but I knew that the Kid would see no sense in my having myself killed under the circumstances.

I went over to the workbench and watched. They were dressing him in his best clothes. I thought: So long Kid. I won't be seeing much of you after this.

He looked in a way I have always remembered. His face was not pale but reddish, with the thin skin that burned so easily, and the light lashes which were sometimes invisible, and the small reddish ears, but I suppose the candles might have given him some of that color. He was a nice-looking kid, all right, and I could see why the senoritas had gone for him. He had those slate-colored eyes and the golden eyebrows and the brown-golden cropped head and the good nose and bright teeth and the strong fast body. And of course his smiling and laughing all the time had pleased them. You would have thought they would not have gone for his red-rimmed eyes and the thin burned skin that never turned brown but the senoritas liked him for his coloring, he was so different from the fellows they knew. He was still laughing now. The little laughter muscles around his nostrils and mouth were pinched and the curves around his mouth had broken out and you could catch a glimpse of his teeth, with the slightly purple lips around them. Someone had closed his eyes, which had been open in Hijinio's adobe, and I was glad.

They dressed him in a white shirt, Francesca at the last minute swabbing down the front of his chest, and they fixed a black string tie on him and drew on a dark jacket and then they placed lighted candles all around him and sat down and began to weep. Some of the paisanos came in and watched, not saying much, only a few words now and then behind a hand, and looking sad. Nobody said anything at all to me. After a while I got tired of this and I thought, Well so long Kid, and I went out and went down to the rocks jutting out toward the seawolves.

They are strange rocks down there, in places sharp as

knives. I had to be careful in my bare feet. As I went down from the hill where the meadow is I saw the small spired windcut castles, strong in the moonlight, and behind them the hill and behind that, across the cove, the cypress grove. I saw the little beach on my left below me and went down on the hard rocks with the stones jutting out, the stones that looked burned through, and I heard a gull cry. And all the time I heard the seawolves barking and snarling, the sound coming in with the wind, and now and again I heard the women crying up in the barn.

I went down to the flat-lying smooth rocks which looked like big aprons tilting into the sea, and I could feel the ripples of their muscles against my feet and the lacy patterns where the tides had eaten them, and then I went to the left to the cutting rocks again and climbed down among them and jumped the small fiord and crawled out to the outermost rocks, the steel rocks like knives, which I would have thought had come from an earthquake but which Francesca said had been an old river bed, and I sat there looking out toward the seawolves and thinking nothing. Now I could not hear the women crying. I heard the wind and the waves and the seawolves snarling and I thought of nothing.

Then I thought, Well so long Kid, and began to think of leaving in the morning. Then I wondered what Nika was doing. I wondered if she were still lying there like that, naked, and if any of the men had gone in and seen her, and if Francesca had covered her. Then I heard a noise behind me and I saw her coming, the other side of the fiord, wearing a thin old dress.

"Nika," I said.

She stopped. When she saw me she turned around and went back.

"Nika," I said, but she kept going. "Have it your own way," I said.

I would have followed her but I was too tired. What was the use of it anyway? I wouldn't have slept with her even if I could have, not on that night, not while the Kid was lying all dressed up in the barn. But her coming there had spoiled the spot for me and I got up and climbed back. I slipped once and cut my left heel and cussed. I saw the castles again and heard some gulls and saw two pelicans flying across the cove and saw the whole placing swimming in moonlight and I climbed up to the meadow and as I walked through the meadow I decided to have me a couple of drinks. I went into my place and had them out of the bottle and then I went into the Kid's.

She was still lying on the bunk where I had left her, her elbows across her face. She had not left the bed. It had been some other girl who had come down to the rocks.

"Nika," I said.

She uncovered her face and looked at me. Her face was stained with tears.

"He was my compadre," I said.

She only looked at me. It was not a hard look and not a soft one.

"I'm leaving in the morning," I said.

She just looked at me with those sunken eyes, her cheek-bones very sharp and high.

"Nika," I said.

She kept looking at me.

"I'm lonely Nika," I said.

She covered her face again and I went out and went over to the barn. The Kid still lay there, with the tallow candles around him. Jesús Garcia, who had killed the yearling and was a pretty good carpenter, was nailing together a coffin out of some old boards. I watched him. When he finished, he and I lifted the Kid and put him inside. Francesca began crying and said, "My poor boy, my poor Chivato." Jesús Garcia nailed down the boards and he and I and two other fellows carried the coffin out to the grove and there, in the little opening near the ghost tree, the very old tree without leaves, the tree with the weathered greens and blues and the burning rust, we buried him. Jesús Garcia had made a little cross, which he stuck at the head of the grave. Longworth and his deputies had joined the small group and they stood there with their hats in their hands, but their hands low to be near their guns.

Then we all went back to the barn and Longworth had his inquest. It said something about how these fellows, Mexicans, had heard that Hendry Jones had been killed in the house of one Hijinio Gonzales on the Punta del Diablo and how they had proceeded to the said house and found the said Hendry Jones, alias the Kid, with a bullet in his chest above the heart. How they had heard Hijinio Gonzales' story and how this story told of the killing of Hendry Jones by Samuel Longworth, sheriff. And how they, the jury, found that the act of the said Longworth was justifiable homicide. There were six in the jury but only two could sign their names to the paper, the others putting down exes. The paper was written by Hijinio and handed to Dad. Now that he had it, Dad could leave.

He and his deputies went out and mounted their horses. They were about to ride off when one of the fellows of the jury—I don't remember who—went up to the head of Dad's horse and said:

"Is it true you cut off the Kid's trigger finger?"

This fellow had been conferring with the others and so Dad looked at them all.

"Hombre," he said quietly, "are you loco?"

Webb said, "Go on give them the finger Dad."

"Yes," said the man. "Give it to us."

Dad looked hard at them, then said: "What would I want with his trigger finger? Don't you know that I liked him? That I was once his pard? That the only reason I killed him was because it was a groundhog case of him or me?"

One of the men said to Francesca, "Did you see the trigger finger on his hand?"

She thought, then shrugged one shoulder.

The man asked another woman, "Did you see the trigger finger?" She also thought, then shrugged.

The men conferred and decided to dig the Kid up. I went up to my place and strapped on my gunbelt and returned as they were about to start digging.

"Hombres," I said.

They turned around and looked at me.

"If you had asked me I would have told you," I said. "Nobody took his finger."

"You know nothing about it," one of them said.

"Hombres," I said. "Don't dig him up. He was my compadre."

"Some compadre," one of them said.

"Hombres I ask you," I said.

"No," said the man.

I shrugged. "Then I'll kill the first man who touches his grave with a spade," I said.

They looked at each other and then looked at Longworth, but Dad only took a deep drag on his cigarette and said nothing. The men threw down their spades.

One of them said, "I think I saw his trigger finger."

Francesca said, "Yes it was on his hand."

Dad was about to ride off.

Then somebody said, "It wasn't the Kid who got killed. The Kid got away to old Mex. It was a fellow looks like the Kid. They couldn't kill the Kid that way. The Kid's in old Mex having himself a time."

Longworth shook his head unbelievingly. "What a loco bunch," he said.

The fellow asked Francesca, "Do you think it was the Kid?"

"How should I know?" she said.

"Hombres," I said, "don't disturb his grave."

"We won't," said one. "Because it's not the Kid."

Dad wheeled his horse.

"Come on," he said to his deputies. "Before I go loco too. I got some sleeping to do."

They trotted off towards the mission road, Dad looking back now and then.

"It wasn't the Kid!" cried one of the men.

And Francesca Zamora said to me, "It's not the Kid. The Kid's in old Mex."

"That's very good Francesca," I said.

About the author

CHARLES NEIDER (1915–2001) was a prolific essayist, novelist, nature writer and Mark Twain scholar. Born in Odessa, his family moved to America when he was five. In addition to Twain, he edited the works of Robert Louis Stevenson, Washington Irving and Leo Tolstoy. *The Authentic Death of Hendry Jones*, first published in 1956, was the basis of the only film directed by Marlon Brando, *One-Eyed Jacks*.

More from Apollo

THE LOST EUROPEANS
Emanuel Litvinoff

> *Coming back was worse, much worse, than Martin Stone had*
> *anticipated.*

Martin Stone returns to the city from which his family was
driven in 1938. He has concealed his destination from his
father, and hopes to win some form of restitution for the
depressed old man living in exile in London. *The Lost Europeans*
portrays a tense, ruined yet flourishing Berlin where nothing
is quite what it seems.

BOSNIAN CHRONICLE
Ivo Andrić

> *For as long as anyone could remember, the little café known as*
> *'Lutvo's' has stood at the far end of the Travnik bazaar, below the*
> *shady, clamorous source of the 'Rushing Brook'.*

This is a sweeping saga of life in Bosnia under Napoleonic
rule. Set in the remote town of Travnik, the newly appointed
French consul soon finds himself intriguing against his
Austrian rival, whilst dealing with a colourful cast of locals.

THE MAN WHO LOVED CHILDREN
Christina Stead

> *All the June Saturday afternoon Sam Pollit's children were on the*
> *lookout for him as they skated round the dirt sidewalks and seamed*
> *old asphalt of R Street and Reservoir Road that bounded the deep-*
> *grassed acres of Tohoga House, their home.*

Sam and Henny Pollit have too many children, too little money and too much loathing for each other. As Sam uses the children's adoration to feed his own voracious ego, Henny becomes a geyser of rage against her improvident husband.

MY SON, MY SON
Howard Spring

> *What a place it was, that dark little house that was two rooms up*
> *and two down, with just the scullery thrown in! I don't remember to*
> *this day where we all slept, though there was a funeral now and then*
> *to thin us out.*

This is the powerful story of two hard-driven men – one a celebrated English novelist, the other a successful Irish entrepreneur – and of their sons, in whom are invested their fathers' hopes and ambitions. Oliver Essex and Rory O'Riorden grow up as friends, but their fathers' lofty plans have unexpected consequences as the violence of the Irish Revolution sweeps them all into uncharted territory.

DELTA WEDDING
Eudora Welty

The nickname of the train was the Yellow Dog. Its real name was the Yazoo-Delta. It was a mixed train. The day was the 10th of September, 1923 – afternoon. Laura McRaven, who was nine years old, was on her first journey alone.

Laura McRaven travels down the Delta to attend her cousin Dabney's wedding. At the Fairchild plantation her family envelop her in a tidal wave of warmth, teases and comfort. As the big day approaches, tensions inevitably rise to the surface.

THE DAY OF JUDGMENT
Salvatore Satta

At precisely nine o'clock, as he did every evening, Don Sebastiano Sanna Carboni pushed back his armchair, carefully folded the newspaper which he had read through to the very last line, tidied up the little things on his desk, and prepared to go down to the ground floor...

Around the turn of the twentieth century, in the isolated Sardinian town of Nuoro, the aristocratic notary Don Sebastiano Sanna reflects on his life, his family's history and the fortunes of this provincial backwater where he has lived out his days. Written over the course of a lifetime and published posthumously, *The Day of Judgment* is a classic of Italian, and world, literature.

NOW IN NOVEMBER
Josephine Johnson

> *Now in November I can see our years as a whole. This autumn is like both an end and a beginning to our lives, and those days which seemed confused with the blur of all things too near and too familiar are clear and strange now.*

Forced out of the city by the Depression, Arnold Haldmarne moves his wife and three daughters to the country and tries to scratch a living from the land. After years of unrelenting hard work, the hiring of a young man from a neighbouring farm upsets the fragile balance of their lives. And in the summer, the rains fail to come.